MAGNETISM

Books by Jacqueline Gay Walley

'Venus As She Ages' Collection of Novels:
Strings Attached (Second Edition, Gay Walley)
To Any Lengths
Prison Sex
The Bed You Lie In
Write, She Said
Magnetism

Books by Gay Walley

Novels:
Strings Attached (First Edition)
The Erotic Fire of the Unattainable
Lost in Montreal
Duet

E-Books on Bookboon:
The Smart Guide to Business Writing
How to Write Your First Novel
Save Your One Person Business From Extinction

Amazon Chap-Books:
How to Be Beautiful
How to Keep Calm and Carry On Without Money

MAGNETISM
A NOVEL

Jacqueline Gay Walley

PUBLICATIONS

Book Six of the VENUS AS SHE AGES *Collection*

I have lived many of the places I write about, many of these characters are based on real people, alive or dead, and I occasionally even use real names, so it is understandable people may think these are real stories. But this book is a work of fiction, because all the events and places got transmuted into a fictitious story that the real people would not even recognize. In addition, just as many of the characters are fictitious, the events are fictitious, perhaps even my analyses in the books are fictitious. That said, it bears repeating that nothing in the novel is intended as a recounting of actual events. Apart from the broad parallels, this is not what actually happened to me, nor to the people I write about.

Copyright © 2021 by Jacqueline Gay Walley
www.gaywalley.com

Published by IML Publications LLC
www.imlpublications.com

Distributed worldwide by Ingram Content Group
www.ingramcontent.com

Book cover design and interior layout by Erin Rea
www.erinreadesign.com

Cover Image: Alamy B0K3WH
Roman goddess, Venus Genetrix', c1518-1574
Artist: Maerten van Heemskerck

ISBN: 978-1-955314-14-5

Library of Congress Control Number: 2021941312

IML Publications LLC
151 First Avenue
New York City, NY 10003

This book is dedicated to Vicki Abrams for so kindly being there emotionally, physically and in every way, helping me to realize my dreams.

CHAPTER 1

As before any date, Mira began by dressing. Yes, she was going to be by herself but what was wrong with that black lace dress that was totally impractical with its long zipper in the back and quite low cut in front (why had she bought it she wondered)? It was a part of her, a part of her young and a part of her now that she is not young and she would wear it. Stockings, boots, and she'd do her hair.

Part one of her date would involve the Highline. The last time she walked it, she had been with a 14-year-old student. He had been wondering if he should adopt a literal black sheep so it would not get killed in a slaughterhouse. An unusual question and therefore thrilling. So as they weaved through the walkway and the Hudson River on one side of them, on these very railroad tracks that were built to take animals to slaughter (and had that conversation been a coincidence? Now it seems impossible that it was not but had she been so drugged on the day, the sun, her fondness for this young boy that she had not put that together then?), she had cursorily looked at the elegant plantings along the walkway, the trellises of vines, the rows of proudly just potted trees with their almost silver green leaves, the wild weeds that the landscapers had allowed, even enabled, to live on the Highline. That day she had walked with her student; they had imagined him reading his poetry right here, with his black sheep. It had seemed one of the better ways to spend one's time. It would cost $20 a week to save the sheep, he said, but then where would one keep it? He couldn't see it in his mother's back yard.

It was not lost on her or him who exactly were the black sheep. Their hearts had gone out over the Highline horizon, yearning for that black sheep's life.

She hadn't been to the Highline since.

How long since she'd taken a walk with herself? How bloody long?

Fortunately it was still warm outside. So she grabbed a cab to 14th to save time and climbed the stairs to the park. The name of the park always sounded like the name of a bar to her.

The Highline. She began to breathe.

Once again it was crowded as if with the same people as when she had been there before. She milled among the crowds busy taking photographs and sitting on those wooden slat benches, tourists, men without shirts, older people like herself except she didn't yet consider herself old and she bought herself an apple pie fruitsicle, after all she was on a date. Her high heel slipped into the slat between the wooden floorboards and some man complimented her quick recovery. All around were the burgeoning high rise, ultra expensive buildings popping up like beanstalks, but still, still there was the art of this building next to that building, the counterpoint so to speak, the whole place was built on counterpoint, gardens over tracks, looking over an industrial New Jersey, an industrial New York disappearing to shops and instantaneous glass buildings built with touches of blue.

Everything was quite the same except she was alone. She had debated asking Kurt, her so-called boyfriend, to join her and the real reason she didn't, is he would have said no. He was not in love with her, he liked to tell her, and he certainly wasn't enough to race to see her whenever there were a few free moments. Other men had been but he wasn't. Those other relationships hadn't worked out so she was confused as to exactly what did constitute a healthy relationship. Strangely Kurt and she lasted, as long as she was willing to exist on minimal attention.

A fact that continually grated on her.

She looked around. Did people look happy walking the Highline? Not really, but probably they were. Sometimes they stopped to look at the view of the Hudson, or to look for their other half to pass on another comment from where to have dinner to how quickly the sun was setting. She sat down and faced the street and its old and new buildings, not the river. It was warmer here and no one was on this bench. She needed privacy for this date. So far all this date was proving that it is better not to date alone.

Her next stop was the Strand. The Village Voice had listed it as the best place to pick up women. This amused her. There were long gone days where men had tried to pick her up in bookstores. She used to say to them, Don't judge a book by its cover. She seemed to remember they quickly got into discussing getting under the covers. She wasn't sure. It had been a long time since anyone had tried to pick her up anywhere. She didn't even hope for it anymore.

She walked along the street, feeling slightly faint. Was it the weight of being alone? The sadness of going on a date with, of all the reckless and inconstant people in the world to choose from, she ends up with herself.

She'd been here just last week with the same student she'd walked the Highline with. He is now 17. He is in love with words as she was at 17. So she had decided to direct him to writers in love with words. She got Henry Miller for him, Bukowski, Bolano. Tall and handsome, the boy followed her through the stacks. He loved that she was taking seriously "the banned books" section. It was all new to him. She gave him a little smile. As she amassed the books for him, one of the salesmen came up to her and said, "I love your taste."

The student had texted her that night, reading Miller. "I'm crazy about him."She had been too at that age.

Now, alone, she looked around. *The Goldfinch* everywhere. She hadn't been able to get through it. What with all those words? Markson gone from prominence, now that he is dead and not advocating for himself. (Is that what will happen to her and why should she care?) The Brooklyn boys like Lethem. She liked to see what the staff recommended. It was like listening to gossip.

"Oh I remember you," the young salesman sidled up to her, wearing a big beige sweater, and now that he was close, she caught the retro smell of cigarettes.

She smiled. "Why don't you carry Markson anymore?"

"Must not sell. How about Whitehead?" he asked. "Like him?"

"Some. I like how he interprets happiness," she said, "as embracing change, risk. Pretty cool for an Oxford or Cambridge mathematician."

"Wild," he said. "Where's your friend?"

He meant her student. "I am sure we'll be in. But soon he's off to college."

She looked at this young man who must wonder why she would be wistful about a young person's liberation.

"Well, need anything in particular today?" he asked.

"I don't think so," she said. "But thanks."

He nodded and, like an apparition, retreated into a maze of books.

She decided to leave. So much for that part of her date, a brief chat with a Marlboro smoking denizen of paperbacks.

What should she do next that might feel less lonely? All art aspires to the condition of music. Was that Santayana or Pater? Who knows? Her date, like Juliette Binoche in the movie *Blue,* would be music.

She had done much worse many times before.

For some reason, she loved sitting on the parquet, no matter that it did not quite match her finances. Tonight was Mahler and Mozart. She had never liked Mozart, too chirpy, too happy for her. To express that opinion was often to lose people's respect in minutes. The three staples of tradition: God, Taxes and Mozart.

James Levine, the conductor, heroic in his wheelchair, as if it was a chariot, wheeled himself onto the stage and was lifted up onto a conductor's podium over the orchestra, like a Greek god, by a special contraption built for him. The audience looked on in awe and inspiration. Mira watched their yearning eyes looking to ingest the same strength he had, while noting that she was surrounded by older women like herself, for the very same reason she was there. For passion.

These women came in pairs and talked with each other at intermission. They were dressed of course as old ladies should be dressed, in buttoned up blouses, jackets, no lipstick. Mira sat there, as usual inappropriately, dressed as if she was an understudy for a Sophia Loren film. It made her laugh at herself to see her black lace sleeves as she turned the pages of her program. Autoeroticism. A life of autoeroticism—writing, going to music alone, phone calls.

Like the phone call she had had yesterday with Ian telling her he might live with his ex-girlfriend since the girlfriend told him she might kill herself because she was so broke. She owns a 300,000-dollar condo, he added, which made Mira wonder about the word broke.

Suicide, everyone's secret friend.

Mahler's own death march, with its haunting percussion, was rising and rising now . . . absorbing her and, as always with death, and on a date, even with herself for that matter, her mind turned to sex. Ah, it still could, she noted happily. As the pulsing of the music grew, her mind went to Kurt's perfect bedroom, its exquisite sheets and the city out there behind the blinds and how, once they were naked and sort of snuggling, he moved her hand down from his shoulder to his penis. It was the first movement.

She would then begin playing her own driven music, in time, stimulating him, gently, accurately, and lovingly, with "your little fingers," as he called them, or with her mouth.

She did get a thrill in giving him pleasure, even though she complained about his sexual selfishness to friends. As Mahler was breaking into his own driven melody she remembered making love with another man in the past who had given her pleasure, lovely, but, let's face it, it did not forge any long term connection. Nothing changed except perhaps she slept better. Desire is often more exciting than having to deal with the prize.

She liked how Kurt and Mahler were insistent. Isn't that what she was trying to do now?

The final movement which could make her cry, the long whisper of death, Levine was in perfect time but not in perfect spirit for . . . the timing was more perfect than the meaning and so she was not undone by that movement, as she always hoped for. She stood up to leave. The audience going mad for the performance and yes, yes, why not, it was wonderful but she decided to not stay for the second performance which was the audience's response, their chance to be heard, and she began walking up the aisle.

"What do you think about a drink?"

She turned around and it was a man clutching his program, slightly disheveled, but obviously a man of mind. He was tall, grey-haired, with a slight irony to his eyes. He said, "I know you. I'm a member of the Mahler Society. I've seen you there."

Those nuts, she thought, but she'd never had a great track record of saying no to nuts. In fact, they seemed to be her preference. And a woman on a date, even with herself, should have a drink.

"Okay," she said.

He led her (surprisingly) to the Empire Hotel and to their dark and rather noisy bar. As they walked, she asked, "Did you like the concert?"

"Yes, I enjoyed it but the press will find fault with Levine's predictability. But he didn't maul the piece like I've heard so often."

The bar was full of young women. Young women. That was what her so-called boyfriend Kurt preferred. Or so she imagined, or maybe she simply would have preferred to be one of them herself. She looked over at the Mahlerite or Mahlerian, whatever they call themselves, and he was standing in line at the bar. She sort of liked the energy of him.

Her eyes traveled again to the loud laughter of the young women. They were almost neighing, she thought. And yet they were like sylphs, too.

Did Kurt imagine she was their age, as he kept his eyes shut tight, with her on top of him? Probably, she thought, looking around the bar at these young women with no fat and glowing skin, because she too imagined she was one of them when she was on top of him. She tried to imagine herself as desirable.

"Here," he handed her an old fashioned. "Who drinks those? I think my parents did."

He then began talking about the motives in the symphony and, by accident, kicked her leg, and since she was bored listening to the motives in the Mahler symphony, the technicalities of music were not an obsession for her, her mind traveled, dammit, maybe for the warmth of it against the starkness of dissecting music like it was a lab rat, her mind gave her the image of Kurt throwing his leg over her back when they sleep. It was not the most comfortable but it was his version of putting his arms around her.

She looked back to the man she was with and saw he had a sweet face, although angular. "What are you thinking?" he broke into his monologue.

Kurt had never asked her that, ever.

"About motives," she answered.

"You mean mine? I think you're probably lovable."

Now there's an unusual answer, she thought.

"Why did you go to the symphony alone?" he asked.

"Well you're alone," she said.

"Oddballs like me often go to things like this alone. Women dressed up like you aren't usually alone."

"I'm on a date."

"What happened?"

"A date with myself."

He looked at her quizzically. "How do you like the company?" he asked.

"Not that much. I'm glad I was interrupted."

He looked round the bustling dark room, somewhat impatiently. Kurt would have been sizing up the women's bodies, even in their clothes. "God it's so noisy here," the Mahlerian said. "Who knew?"

It was true. One had to shout to be understood.

"Let's go to a coffee shop," she said, "or somewhere quiet."

Now they were walking outside. The night was gentle and welcoming. "I remember a couple," she said, "I never met them but they too were looking for somewhere quiet."

He looked over at her with a furrowed brow, as if she might

be about to tell him something painful. She interpreted that to mean that more than a few women had been critical of him.

She continued, "I had gone to see a late movie across the street from where I live. In other words, I took a ten-foot journey to *The Hundred-Foot Journey* film, do you remember it?"

He shook his head. Maybe he didn't go to romantic movies like that. Maybe he was always alone. Can't be, she thought.

She continued, "The movie looked innocuous enough. The theater was completely empty, dark. I sat near the front so I didn't have to walk far into the blackness. The film began."

Now he was smiling, safe that this little journey did not have anything to do with him.

"Anyway then I heard a woman moaning and sighing, building into a breathless orgasm, behind me. Way behind me. I looked around furtively and barely made out a man and what I thought was a woman lying across him and I was not sure what exactly they were doing to achieve those sounds, but my imagination quickly filled in lots of blanks, but it was very erotic listening to them, and interesting," she went on, "now that I think about it how the mind instantly sends pictures of what it thinks others are doing." She was silent, ruminating for a second, on how we humans are so predictable. "Anyway, they were looking for somewhere quiet."

He too was silent for a few moments wondering, she assumed,

what she was trying to tell him. What was she trying to tell him?

"Perhaps they were married to other people and too poor to go anywhere else," he said, finally.

"Or perhaps they were exhibitionists and always pick public places to be with each other."

"Perhaps they were so taken with each other," he said, "they could not stop themselves from this happening everywhere they went. Their entire world was their bedroom."

Ah for those days, she thought. "Perhaps," she said evenly so as not to betray that thought itself was rather erotic. The thought immediately had her conjuring up those times when she had made love with men in the past in gardens when at someone's party, bathrooms, probably movies, now that she thought about it.

How could she bring that back? she wondered.

"Anyway, this story is off," she said. "They were not looking for quiet, I realize. They were looking for privacy. Because, as the movie continued, quiet did not seem to be a value they aspired to."

"Then what happened?"

She smiled. A question a child might ask.

"Did you ever see them?" he asked.

"I left quickly after the real movie and went home. But I never forgot it."

"That's the story?"

He looked a bit confused. What was the point? She suddenly remembered: men need a point.

Anyway he was right. That wasn't the story. Now she knew why she had just remembered and recounted it. "Maybe not," she said. "That was the night I decided I didn't want to be alone anymore."

CHAPTER 2

This she found this morning in one of her books, an early one. She reread it to remember that self she was, that self who wore black pants and a velvet halter top on an unusually warm winter day, that woman who had been desirable. She remembered she'd parked in the parking lot of FCI Fort Dix and waited.

"He was supposed to walk out and be cleared around ten a.m. It was only marijuana growing, stupid but not violent, yet it was the Rockefeller laws and he had served ten years in a Federal prison.

He was not her boyfriend when he went in, just an old friend she had known for many years, but incomparably handsome and creative. His sculpture had won him grants, he had purple hearts from Vietnam, he had made $50,000 a week with his marijuana business, in other words, he was a character and she had been fascinated at the trajectory of his life and they had written letters and had many visits and soon the whole impossibility of never having sex made the whole thing impossibly sexy.

Ten years had ended and she was picking him up to drive him to the halfway house. She no longer had a husband and he certainly did not have a girlfriend yet.

Then she saw him tall, in a white t-shirt, slacks, walking through the cars, looking for her blue Escort, ten years since she had seen him walking outside of a contained visiting room. Here he was in normal clothes, nobody around him, carrying the paintings he had done in prison in a roll and his duffel bag.

"Hey baby," he said, laughing, as she jumped out of the car, standing in the sunlight.

She didn't know what to say.

"My god," she said. "Are you sure you don't want to go back in?"

"Let's get out of here."

They drove and he looked out the window, hard. They held hands. "Do you want a coffee? Something?" she asked.

"No thanks."

"I'll take you to lunch after you see my place," she said, "somewhere nice in the city."

He had often talked about hating the food in prison. "Last night," he told her, "the Italian guys made a huge dinner with white napkins as a goodbye party for me. Tomatoes. It was something. I wonder where they got the vegetables."

She smiled.

She knew pretty soon they would see the back of the Statue of Liberty and she had always cried when she passed it returning from visiting him. Sometimes she had been so turned on by being locked up in the visiting room with him, his hard body as they say, his romantic words, his charm and intelligence, that driving home from a visit she had masturbated in the car. One time she had been thrown out of the visiting room for the way his big hand kept stroking her back, her neck, her legs.

"Do you think we have chemistry?" he'd once asked her.

They parked and she brought him upstairs. He walked through her old apartment like it was a palace. He looked out the windows. He took it all in. They hugged. They kissed. And they went to her bedroom. He undressed her, on top of the comforter. He began kissing her body. He was big and in perfect shape and she was happy he was finally here in her arms, naked.

"I can't fucking believe it," he said.

"Don't worry about it."

"Never happened to me before."

"Don't worry about it. Everything is so loaded. You're probably in some kind of shock. Anyway ten years of foreplay has a touch of pressure," she said.

Then she suggested the urban solution to all problems, "Come on let's go to a restaurant. We can table this," she said laughing. "Believe me I am not too worried."

They dressed. Apparently in the old days before he went to prison they'd had sex together in their twenties but she hardly remembered it. She only recalled how he had left her a poem the next morning on the typewriter that faced out over an ever-changing grey and blue sea. She never forgot his handwriting and the fact he would do that. She didn't remember him in bed. And, for obvious reasons, actual sex had never been a big part of their current relationship, with her visiting him once a month in prison. Just sex in the mind and she often wondered if she preferred it that way anyway.

She took him to Il Cantinori, on Tenth. Enormous flower arrangements, windows over the streets, white tablecloths, even for lunch. It was elegant and he had salmon and wine and her best friend who knew him too showed up with clothes for him and even underwear and she wondered about that but they were all excited about his freedom and seeing him out of prison khakis and what was he going to do and he gave many unrealistic answers and nobody cared, just the happiness at all of them never having to see that prison again.

After the dessert, the gaiety, she said, "I've gotta drive you to Boston now. You have to be there by sundown."

Once they retrieved his duffel bag, she and he got back in the car and they drove the long way from New York. They held hands and he talked about how much he loved her and what their future would be. That she was the one and she didn't really believe it but she was like that with all men anyway, she didn't believe much of what any of them said, not because she thought they were lying but she knew how very much everything changes.

They got to Lowell where the halfway house was; they got there early. No way he was going to check in a second before he had to.

"What shall we do?"

"Let's park in that bar's parking lot down the street."

They did and that's when she ended up on top of him in her tiny car, making love with him, lustfully, passionately, happily, who cared who could see them, nobody seemed to be out in Lowell on a weekday afternoon in this part of town and all systems worked as they say and years later he gave her a framed photo of that parking lot as a gift.

They had a passionate affair, but they did not really get on, she was too serious and he was a bit of a wheeler-dealer and so they once again became friends, just as they had been during those ten years of visits, and twenty years of youth before.

CHAPTER 3

This time she wore a dress that she wasn't sure about, it was a dress that reflected the other side of her, her timidity, not form fitting, flowing, as if she was hiding excess weight. It was ironic that here she gets conservative since tonight was a date with an actual man, not herself. But still . . . she was not sure what she wanted with this Mahlerite. They were going to the Second together. Well, you can't beat that. And he mentioned he had good seats.

"But we should have dinner first," he said. "Meet me at Brasserie Cognac."

She had been there before and hadn't liked it much, an American version of a French bistro which often was just a little too large, a little too busy trying to be French, but tonight, maybe it was where he was sitting, it felt more relaxed. She ordered a strong drink and he had wine. He spoke of friends and events he had gone to that week, a reunion, he had looked at his old house in Brooklyn, and she was slightly bored.

They were both holding back. Maybe they both unconsciously knew the event of the evening was the music, and they were not competing with it.

The box at Carnegie Hall was beautiful and he had got her a seat in the front so she had a complete view of the orchestra. The enormous Westminster Chorus sat as one giant wave, taking up the whole back half of the stage. The music began and as the first three notes were played, she and her date finally smiled at each other, their blood starting to flow in a way that Mahler's openings did for them. Now he and she were as one. Many times at music she went into herself but this performance she remained, eyes open, riveted to the stage. She in a way missed her usual time for introspection but the pride with which the drummers picked up their sticks and the way they gave their whole bodies to all the different variations of beat seemed to have some life lesson for her, if she could figure it out. Between movements, she turned back to her date, who also was overcome. One movement after the next was ungluing her. It was as if her soul was being undressed one page of music at a time.

There were Mahlerites spread throughout the audience and sometimes she looked to them to see how they were responding. Some were completely held, others she imagined were cataloging what the conductor was doing wrong. Most of them, she knew, considered themselves to be the reigning world expert on Mahler.

Who was Mahler? Tonight she wondered if he was a god.

By the time the last movement unfolded, she was crying. After the final note, the audience jumped up screaming in applause. She too stood, arms raised, vigorously clapping, and hoped the conductor would single out the players who had been so extraordinary but he did not and she wondered if that was his exhaustion or that no musician, to him, was greater than the other.

When it all ended, she followed her date out of the box and she sure as hell did not want to make banal conversation. Fortunately he was silent, too.

She remembered at that moment why she had not been able to commit to the prisoner. He had not surprised her enough in conversation. Really? Would she do that? End a relationship over a person's ability for invention? Would she keep a relationship going simply because she didn't know what a man's next sentence would be?

Finally outside in a light dusting of rain, after both of them seemed to make a private, painful readjustment to what world they were living in anyway, "Want to have a drink?" he asked.

"No, I'll be drunk."

He scratched his head.

"Want to come to my place?" he ungracefully asked.

She was taken aback. "Where do you live?"

He pointed to a building across the street. Seemed a bit upscale for one of the Mahlerians who struck her as types who grew, like mushrooms, in subterranean places. They did not seem to live in the pan and gloss of the real world.

"Okay."

They walked into an elegant lobby. "Good evening Mr. Puccini."

In the elevator, "Mr. Puccini?" she asked.

"He knows I like music and the only composer he seems to know is Puccini."

She smiled. She liked that he didn't seem insulted or put out by it.

She had never asked him his last name. He looked Jewish, not Italian, although the prisoner used to call Italians, "Silly Jews."

He was opening the door to his apartment and she knew this had often been the moment of truth. This is where you learn if the man only has prints when he can afford real art, or where there are not enough books, or no light, that in particular had often done her in, even when she didn't want it to. She was pretty sure there would be lots of music.

They walked into what felt like a white open room with many windows, simple, lots of books and lots of paintings and photographs. Not too neat, a newspaper here, there, he obviously had not been preparing to bring her back. The furniture was a type of Danish, she thought, but what was best, were his passions. A photo of a Greek fresco. A bust of a composer but not Mahler. She looked at it. "Scriabin," he said.

"Oh."

"In college, I listed my name in the phone book under Scriabin."

She smiled. "Did you get a lot of calls?"

"Not even from girls I wanted to like me."

Then she noticed the books were chemistry. Also rather global. "What did you do for work?" she asked. "Or do?"

"These," he pointed to the chemistry, "were when I taught."

"High school?"

"No. Harvard. And these," he pointed to the global, "is when I did . . . other things."

"Like what?"

"Like working for multinationals in research."

"A brain," she said.

He left the room and went and got some Courvoisier. She

didn't think people still drank Courvoisier.

"I used to drink these in Montreal," she said. "But nobody I know does anymore."

He made no comment, just looked at her.

She was thinking he wasn't bad. It seemed there would be enough to explore in him. And he wasn't doing any selling.

"What are you thinking about?" he asked.

"You. That you're . . . there's more than meets the eye."

"I should hope so," he answered.

"I was also thinking how I get drained by things that are not unusually good, unlike tonight. If something is mediocre or safe, it has an adverse affect on me."

He stared at her. Then he said, "I don't understand."

"Like as an example, when I have to read work that doesn't feed me. Or engage in conversation that is predictable. Or when I hear music that is not passionate, I don't know, I guess I have been doing too much of all that, I get exhausted."

"Are you saying your palate needs the highest good?" he asked, smiling.

"I am, sadly. I am. Not that I'm the highest good . . ."

"You're probably just saying you need to be loved."

She pursed her mouth together, thinking. She didn't see the connection but she was willing that there could be one. She would parse it later, when she was alone.

"Maybe you're right," she replied.

CHAPTER 4

She had been teaching all day, ending with a class that finished at 9 pm. A woman her own age had come to the class with lines all over her face and a terribly written story about her own divorce but sporting a huge ring and Mira knew that in some way this woman was smarter than she was. She had found committed love.

Mira left the class feeling love, too, but for all her students, profound love, for their dedication to words, to making something, to effort. And their beauty. Most of them had unblemished faces, heavy natural eyelashes, lively smiles. She herself was a bit in love with their beauty, which embarrassed her.

And then she grabbed a cab to Kurt's penthouse.

The doorman let her up and Kurt was waiting at the apartment door. It was too late for dinner and she didn't want any anyway, there had been too many dinners lately with too many people she had found boring and when she did, she ate the bread or had a second drink because she was just so uninterested in the conversation, or was it lack of sexual energy, and so all she wanted now was a scotch by his fireplace.

He opened the door, smiling. "Did you have a tough day, honey?" he joked and then laughed.

She could see flames in the fireplace. "Oh," she said, thrilled, "a fire . . ."

And he had a bottle of scotch out on the dining room table and two glasses with ice and he poured them long scotches and then they both sat down by the fire, he across from it on his blue divan and she on the fire place itself, looking back at him. She wanted the warmth on her spine.

They began to chat. He had played tennis the night before with the son of a friend of hers who had recently died and he'd had lunch with a friend of his who had been in Kurt's business at one time and was now a touch lonely.

"All these mitzvahs," she said.

"Yes the boy was smart, mature and wonderful to be with. James, on the other hand, is a wonderful guy but he keeps repeating the same stories, the very ones he told me the first time he met me."

"Oh," she said.

"He needs to open up his repertoire," he said.

She nodded. Kurt, she found, was quick to find fault with people. But so was she. She just didn't vocalize it as much.

Then she told him of a friend of hers who told her she should marry for money. It had shocked her a bit. It seemed so vulgar.

"It's vaguely insulting," he said, but she wasn't sure her friend had meant it that way.

"Well her husband married money in marrying her," he said.

"No, they love each other."

"They're always traveling about. They must not like being together like we do. We don't need to go places, we just enjoy each other. I give them two years," he said and she laughed.

"Yes, we last—" she said.

"You're tenacious, honey."

"I am," she replied. She liked him using words, and he probably liked the same about her.

"But," he said, "I keep us on course. I have not let you destroy us."

"I thought you said I am tenacious."

"But I am the captain," he said, his eyes laughing.

"You are," she said, although she thought the reason they

had lasted was her ability to put up with him. "And guess what? Alan, after 2 years, called me—"

"Didn't he get married?"

"No, it turns out they broke up."

"Maybe he is interested in you," Kurt said.

"No," she said. "Why would you think that? Anyway he is not my type."

As far as she could see, Kurt turned out to be her type.

She told him about the play she'd seen while he had been playing tennis the other night and that she had found it tedious, even though it is considered by everyone else genius, and he said he'd read about it and knew that it would be tedious and so on.

New York dialogue.

The thing was that when she was with him, the rest of the world did not exist. She did not want to look at her phone, she did not even think about being somewhere else.

Just the fire in the fireplace and him.

Eventually they went downstairs to bed and both remarked on Gore Vidal being on Charlie Rose, "He's a good writer," she said (someone had written a biography of him) and Kurt said, "A smart man," and then she ascertained Vidal's politics must be closet conservative since Kurt's were, very, and he went off to his bathroom and she got into bed and surfed for something magical, which is impossible on TV, and she found the movie, *Striptease,* he would like that, she thought, and he did for a bit, not the stripping but the campiness of the script and then they made love, and she did not feel young and lithe because she wasn't, and so making love almost hurt her emotionally, but at the end it began to feel good physically and then it was over and they immediately fell asleep.

CHAPTER 5

Her seventeen-year-old student had come with her to buy him more books by Roberto Bolano and Jonathan Lethem. He had put his arm out for her to hold onto as they walked to the Strand. She was struck by how soft his skin was. After they shopped, she wanted to go home and he was going off, he said, to make conversation with his Mennonite girlfriend's parents at her soccer game. He was dreading it. Mira made the assumption that her parents did not like him because he was black. Her heart broke at his tall, earnest beauty as he walked off.

Ah well, any pain is good for a writer, she told herself. Eventually. And, so far, it seemed this boy was going to be a writer.

She did not sleep with the Mahlerian because of Kurt. At this late age, she rued to herself, she goes all honest and moral. Or maybe she was not attracted to him. There was something staid about his world and she had always avoided the staid. The bookstore denizen had been right about loving Whitehead. Whitehead said evolution must be change.

You learn as you get older sex is sacred. The number of people she had slept with whose names she could not remember or anything of interest about them, those days were over.

Maybe with time being shorter she wanted the whole thing, body, mind and soul. The Mahlerian was playing for that too, she thought, or capable of that. Kurt was playing to be safe or have as many options as he could. It would be a no-brainer for anyone else.

"I have 2 tickets to a piano concert on the 13th," the Mahler goer said to Mira on the phone. "Come."

"I am taking a student's mother out to dinner that night."

"Reschedule her."

Ah, men. It's so simple for them, she thought. They just go right to what they want.

It occurred to her later when she was getting a manicure, being touched so efficiently by young Asian women, that the way to accomplish getting what she wanted was to just say yes.

It was an astonishing thought to her, one she had had before, but one she never paid much attention to.

But she did not cancel her student's mother. Her work life was important to her. Work had been all that she had had as her own. It had had its share of abandonments and embarrassing faux pas, it had had its share of rejections and defeats, and its share of all too brief moments of glory, but it had been constant. It had become less a source of worry over the years even though she had become less marketable, but in response to that, she had been intelligent enough to give herself the pleasure of work she loved in exchange for diminished income.

She read or wrote stories all day. Her own and other people's. Their intensity and their struggles never ceased to amaze her in their similarities. Everyone felt they were disenfranchised. Always these books would save the person. The author would have meaning. What they lived through would have meaning.

It was as if a published book would double the person's size, protect them from their fragility.

She knew nothing doubled one's size except perhaps the feeling of being loved.

But to midwife, to hold a flashlight for someone as they navigate their stories was a kind of gift, one she honored. She was holding people's dreams. She was holding people's hope. It was a terrible responsibility and strangely she had been given the kindness and insight for it.

That said, she needed to make more money. It would be so relieving to not be on the edge all the time. At this last minute, right now, she had to hit home runs. Everywhere. Actually produce materials that rendered income. If that was at all possible. She probably needed to do the same when young, gain some stability, but she just never thought about it, so absorbed was she by a self defeating need for love.

But usually her mind still froze at the whole wrestling with it.

Which led her to walk up the stairs to her neighbor, Lucia, a holocaust survivor. Mira never expressed to Lucia what she meant to Mira but anyone who could go to a new end of the earth and start again, with a completely shattered heart, and every odd against you because of it, made Mira soar with admiration.

"Come in." The door was always open.

Mira noted, as always, that their apartments were disturbingly similar in taste. A piano, old furniture diffused with art. Books. Music.

"I'm over here," and there she was on the couch with the New York Times. Lucia was very old now, in her late eighties, but still attractive somehow. Full-dyed red hair, elegant clothes. A wonderful quick smile. She was still energetic in her movements, as if she must always be ready, on the alert to outrun fate.

Sitting next to Lucia was a book that Lucia had written. It had just come out about her experiences in the war. Lucia held it up, "Now everyone knows too much about me. Right out for everyone to read and see."

"I think it's really good. You at least are considered too old to do social networking. Not all is lost."

"I was never adept at social networking even in person," Lucia answered. "What's wrong with you?" she asked.

Mira sat down across from her. "The thing about ending up old, broke, alone is you feel so stupid. But it's not like one had a choice. The real tragedy is if you could not put yourself forward in youth…you pay…now. Thus you pay young and you pay old. In the middle you run around with your head cut off. "

Lucia looked down at her newspaper. "Your real problem is you have a boyfriend who doesn't want to kiss you."

Mira ignored that. "What I like about your book, by the way, is that it's vulnerable. And risky. And you just keep going. That is what I like so much. You just kept going."

"Why do you stay with him?" she asked Mira. "You never get to be receptive of love with him…"

"It's not totally true. Last night he took me to the planetarium.

I found that unusual and endearing…"

"He obviously wanted to go there himself."

"Okay," Mira said. "Even if that is true, it's not a crime."

"You don't get to be sheltered, cared for. Does he think about what you need or want? Believe me, I know hunger and know satiety, and I know unkindness, deeply, but each morning I do my hair, wear a dress, and still believe in a kiss, if I am to live fully. It is that kiss that I knew I needed to receive, as I think about it, that was the sign, the sign I would move forward when I arrived. Not waste away from grief. Heed my point."

"I am speaking, Lucia, about finances."

"That is what you think," Lucia said in that clipped Austrian accent that always sounds vaguely annoyed.

Not even her neighbor wanted to think about money. We're a strange lot, Mira thought. But she tried again, "The fact is I'm not qualified for anything remunerative. That's the problem. Not kisses."

"You think I qualified when I arrived here? What were my talents? I first thought I should talk to people and they would tell me what to do. I tried but they seemed so out of it, as if they lived in another universe. I was too tired or broken, what's the difference, to train to be a nurse or a therapist or a teacher. Plenty of people who were high born became cleaning people. I must enter the world from a new door, I told myself."

"And?"

Mira had heard all this before but she always hoped that in every telling there may slip a secret nugget that would pave her own way.

"I did not know much except the vagaries of human nature. Write that on a resume, I told myself. And then do with me what you will."

"That's what you did?" Mira asked.

"I just told you. I wrote on my resume that I only knew the vagaries of human nature and then I said, do with me what you will."

"I find that odd that after life having been quite cruel in doing with you what they will, you would take this approach."

They were silent for a second.

"Not to mention, I find it even stranger that anyone who read your resume could figure out what you were saying," Mira laughed. "Did they?"

"I can't remember. Probably it got me nowhere. Or a typing job with someone equally eccentric," Lucia said. "Alright. Let's be constructive. Let me tell you what you should write about."

"If there is one thing I hate is, people thinking they know what other people should write about."

"Indulge me."

"Okay."

"Write, and god knows it is needed, Venus as she Ages."

Mira laughed. "I didn't know you were so new age."

"Think about it. She did age but there are no images."

"You mean the real Venus?"

"Of course not. I mean all of us."

Mira stood up. This was ridiculous, she thought.

" Ah I struck a chord. Excellent," Lucia said.

"I don't like to write about the obvious."

"Everybody writes about the obvious."

Mira kissed her and said, "Well that's probably true but the trick is to sound fresh. How does one do that?"

"Easy," she said.

"Oh?"

"Believe in love."

Mira sighed. For a minute, she could understand why men find arguing with women so frustrating. We're dogs with bones. "I'll think about it," she answered. "Do you need anything?"

"Only things, which you cannot provide."

"Call me if you need anything which I can."

"I will darling."

CHAPTER 6

Mira hadn't seen Kurt in days. At first, she felt hurt and gaping, abandoned, mistreated, and then it just became how things were.

But maybe feeling hurt was the way things always were. Mira remembered being married and feeling that same slight woundedness, even with her husband loving her. Something he said that she felt was demeaning. Some way he didn't look at her. Some way he walked ahead of her. Tiny cuts that had her feeling, in certain moods, as if she was being bled alive. That was years ago.

Now she went to get her ice skates. It had become almost funny to her to see how difficult it was for her to follow the teacher's directions. But beautiful to be gliding around, next to him as he told her to lower her knees, move her feet sideways, not forward.

The day began like a piece of music, skating, with Sarah Vaughan and Nat King Cole coming through the speakers and the trees and the beauty in Bryant Park. She left the rink feeling happy and it was clear that the secret to all of this was to take on new activities. In that way, she would not think of Kurt so much.

She had written him last night and he responded complaining of insomnia. He told her not to skate, her bones were delicate, he said.

As she went on the Internet that morning, she could not miss all these men marrying women half their age.

A male friend had told her a story. "When I was in college," he said, "I was at a party and I fell for a woman I was watching. She saw me watching her. She was with another guy. At the end of the party I left with my friends and she came out to the parking lot and walked up to my car, and knocked on the window. I rolled it down and she gave me a wonderful kiss and then walked away to her boyfriend.

"That is what I want now," he said. "That feeling."

"Everybody wants that feeling," she answered. "Everyone."

Or did she mean herself? But who wants to be kissed by an older woman?

Was this Kurt's deleterious effect on her?

Venus as she ages.

She rolled around in bed.

And then she dialed the Mahlerian.

"It's Mira."

"You do know it's 3 am?"

"Can I come sleep over? I just can't sleep alone anymore."

"Yes."

As she put a raincoat over her naked body, she smiled as she realized he didn't even hesitate.

He opened his door, naked himself. She was a little stunned and also she liked his height, his long legs. Her father had had long legs. At least they had seemed so to her when she was small. No lights were on and he led her to the bedroom.

She got in next to him and he put his arms around her. Kurt never did that. With Kurt, it was she who put her arms around him. Or she would sleep on her side with her arm around herself. In truth, Kurt had begun to sort of pick up on the idea that arms should be used in bed. He occasionally emulated her actions. And then he forgot.

She sunk into the Mahlerian's arms. She might as well start to think of him with his real name, which is Mark. She has to start calling him, Mark. After all, she is here in his apartment like this. Then she heard, "Do you want to make love?"

"I don't think so. I mean I don't know you."She realized suddenly she had come simply to be held.

She could hear amusement in his voice, "You know me well enough to arrive naked in a raincoat at 3.30 in the morning but not well enough to have sex."

"Exactly."

He laughed. "Women. It's an infallible logic."

"Yes."

"We can try sleeping, I guess," he said.

"Yes, let's try it. I think I just wanted warmth. I'm sorry. I didn't think."

"This isn't you wanting to act out the scene in the movie theatre?"

She hadn't thought of that either. "No," she laughed.

What was she doing? "Let's sleep," she said.

A man comes to the antique shop she owns and takes her away on a bicycle. In real life, he is a friend of hers who is married to someone else, a wonderful friend, and he is pedaling her away from her antique store and he is whisking her along the road and his arms are strong and she is struck by the movement and the safety in his arms on this flying bike in the night, in love with him. Then they are driving in a station wagon and again he is in charge and they are so warm and he is holding her and is loving and so, romantically, they get to the sea.

She woke up. Mark was already out taking a shower and she lay there thinking about this magical loving dream. Mark came back in wearing his underwear. His body was tight and a bit hairy. It was almost a prerequisite with her that a man be hairy.

She could barely stand leaving the dream.

"Did I hold onto you a lot last night?" Mira asked him. She had done so to the bicycling man.

"No," he responded and she closed her eyes. Who was the man on the bicycle?

She had to find him.

It was cool in the bedroom and therefore hard to get out of bed but she forced herself. He was already making coffee in the kitchen. He had put out fruit for her.

She thanked him.

Now what?

They ended up discussing things, none of which she remembered that evening. She only remembered leaning over him, as he was seated, and kissing the side of his face to thank him again.

The next night, he called her. "Want to have dinner?"

"I have to work."

Silence.

"But I'll come over after," Mira said.

That night as she sped over, her heart flying, she knew who the man on the bicycle might be.

He opened the door, smiling. "Well," he said, "you're a cheap date."

He got her a scotch. "Did you eat something?"

"Yes." He handed her a drink.

"God you have to work till 10 at night?" he asked.

"Some students can only come at night."

"Why do you come here and not have me go to your place?" Canny question on his part, she thought. "Are you married?" he asked, joking.

"Yes, to my work. It's strewn all over my apartment. Here, I am on vacation."

She looked out the window at the sea of lights in the city. Biking away to the sea.

She turned to him and felt ensconced. What if she never left here and what if they never talked? She thought about another man she knew who constantly wanted to talk about his mother's narcissism and her father's addictions and why she wouldn't get involved with him, and she had said to him, "It is not a turn on to have you constantly pathologize us."

Mira was sure this man here in this apartment was another child, once time started unraveling things, but for now, for now.

"What do you do all day?" she asked him.

"Drum up money for research on the laser patents I have. Interview post docs to help me. Worry about financing my lab."

"I didn't know you have a lab."

"No, you didn't and I do."

She nodded. "I won't ask what you do because I won't understand it," she said.

"I hardly do myself," he said. "Want to hear some music?"

"No," she said. She didn't like background music with people. She liked the people to be the music.

"Shall we go to bed?" he said.

"Yes."

This was scary, she thought. She must be trying to leave Kurt, trying to find a man who will want her to be in his home, will want more of her than two nights a week. Already Mark had been more enthusiastic about her. Kurt never wanted to see her two nights in a row. He needed to decompress from her, he said. Her very existence must be too much for him.

"You want a t-shirt or something?" he asked in the bedroom.

"No thanks."

He went off into the other room to do whatever he did. She undressed and put her clothes by the bed. She didn't know about anybody else but all she knew was that Kurt never looked at her in bed or out of bed. Once he said as he walked into the bedroom, You look beautiful. Once in six years.

She switched off the light.

He got in. "So here we are," he said.

"Here we are," she answered, smiling.

Did she remember how to kiss? She suddenly wondered. Did he?

"I'm not sure what to do with you," he said.

"Makes two of us."

"But this is the moment of truth. If we don't sleep together, we never will. We will be friends. We are deciding right now the trajectory of our relationship," he said.

He's right, she thought. How many men had she turned into friends. Just this way. No sex. Fidelity to Kurt.

To Kurt who never called her.

Come out of the cocoon, Mira.

She turned to him and put her hands on his chest, then his neck, his face. Could she? Could she begin to know someone else? Come on.

And then she got it. She would do nothing! With Kurt, she

had done everything. She would do nothing.

And he turned to her and began kissing her breasts. "You have lovely nipples," he said.

"And frame," he added.

Is she a house, she wondered. Her eyes flashed to his bedroom window that looked over at other buildings. For a second, she wondered what New York painter this visual reminded her of.

He kept kissing her body. Oh how lovely. And then he pushed her legs apart with his legs, and she touched him and soon he was inside her and nothing terrible happened and she kept telling herself, it's okay, it's okay, and then it was, and after, they held each other and she realized that it would only get better and easier, if she wanted it to. They would slowly begin dismantling their private walls.

And then he said the oddest thing to her. "You got back on the bicycle."

CHAPTER 7

Years ago she did this every night. Walk down steps to a jazz club. When she went to a jazz club, she immediately lost maybe thirty years or more by the time she finally sat down at a table. She knew the music would blow it out of her.

She ordered a drink and began looking around. For some reason, jazz clubs felt like her people, her family. There was an informality she loved and an upcoming attention and absorption. It was sexual. Jazz was sexual and the intensity of hearing it was sexual. It was the same act. And the rivers of feeling.

She pondered it more. One's attention and ear are, she told herself, taken.

She relaxed knowing that was going to happen. She was about to be taken.

The lights went down and the musicians came onto the stage, in polyester shapeless shirts that did not match their slacks, faces unshaven, bodies not buffed at the gym.

How fabulous. Goodbye Wall Street.

The piano player, without any fanfare, sat down and immediately began going into deep and probing places. Mira sat back and closed her eyes and chose to lose herself, taking the notes into her body. Then she sat forward and carefully studied the pianist, as he leaned over the keys with his stomach hanging, he himself in a trance with his coke bottle glasses staring at the wall behind the piano, and she thought how hard his life must be, eking out a living, at the keys, maybe teaching here and there.

The pianist suddenly opened his mouth and told a story about seeing a television show on child starvation in Africa, and it made him compose a piece and then he began to play. The melody was tender, hurt, and powerful.

She was lost, she had no boundaries.

Would she die in a place like this? She'd hear Mahler as she went up to heaven or wherever she was going but jazz, please, for her last moments on earth.

She would have to time her death so that after the jazz, she just went home and died. But, it would be her last act, which of course would change her mind from dying since nothing, nothing was this alive.

Her eyes were still closed. "A first sign of the beginning of understanding is the wish to die," Kafka said. Not die as in the end. Die to what is ended in you.

Jazz, she returned, had the same restorative power for her as being with Kurt does or did, she wasn't sure anymore. It was where she gave herself over. Last night she had seen him, even chosen him over her friends. Her friends didn't like Kurt, they found him selfish and boorish which he is, but he is also light in some way for her. Perhaps how he never claims her, nor interrupts her life in any way. Perhaps how they are not laden down with arguments about how to load the dishwasher or having to visit someone's unseemly relative. Anyway, she had chosen his body over dinner with her friends. Why it was flashing through her mind here she did not know.

Guilt. Like a barnacle.

Kurt had his 25-year-old French chef there at his apartment. She lived in a suite on the downstairs floor, the same floor as his bedroom. She served them exquisite food, wine, everything of the best quality. A young thin girl with light colored hair that flew around her face and Gallic blue eyes that were intelligent. She had dinner with them, she always did, and laughed at all his jokes. Even Mira laughed. It seemed when she had dinner at his apartment, there was always some young chef (they changed frequently due to expiring visas), eyes raised, dazzled, laughing at his jokes. But she had taken to giving up being jealous of his chefs. What was the point? Let him be with them if he wants to be and she can move on. To her Mahlerian or someone who might want her for more than her own chef responsibilities in his bedroom.

Kurt asked Mira to make them drinks while he built a fire. Mira and Kurt sat by his flames and the scent of fir while his chef cooked and she and Kurt chatted about friends, about themselves. It was as if the Mahlerian had never happened. She was drugged by Kurt's physicality and attention, completely absorbed.

At dinner he talked about his problems with work and even the French chef, whose English was not that good, threw in her comments.

He called her a genius in the kitchen.

He called Mira a genius in her work. Thus, that evening, she learned he throws the word around carelessly. Was her whole relationship with Kurt a Zen activity of keeping her pride in check?

In bed, they had their rituals. She searched for a movie that they watched for 15 minutes and then he wanted her to make love with him. His eyes were closed but she studied his face as she was on top of him and she saw joy, at being provided for and safe in that love. But he was too tired to sustain it.

"Maybe you're over me in that way," she said, as she lay back down and brought the sheets and comforter up over them. Maybe she was over him in that way.

"I don't think so," he said.

They fell asleep. In the morning he wanted to again, and she clung to the wonderful strength of his body, and they did make love or rather she did to him, and then she had to run to the gym. They both jumped out of bed at 7.30 a.m.

So many times, even on Valentine's day where he would make a fuss over her, or just in casual conversation, he'd tell Mira as explanation for their longevity as a couple, "The devil you know is better than the devil you don't know." Men, he added, stay with stasis. Why did she then? That she had total freedom with him? That was all she could come up with. "You are in love with him," a friend said. She and Kurt did pleasant things together, she told herself, and pleasant things, she noted, turned out to be an incredible glue.

She sipped her drink in the jazz club and the horns in the band reminded her of Holst's Venus. The energy though was not ethereal, like Holst's Neptune. What a work of genius The

Planets are.

His chef making tomato soup. Rhubarb dessert. You're a genius, he said.

Why was she here at this music alone and had not invited Mark? He probably didn't really like jazz. The cacophony put a lot of people off. For her, it was her terrain. He must understand it, though. Science is alchemy. Art is cacophony.

Kurt told her that her friend whom she had got out of dinner with to have dinner with him was jealous of her. Why would anyone be jealous of poverty and struggle, she wondered.

You are free, he said.

You have eros, another friend said.

She does?

CHAPTER 8

Now she was alone at her desk with her PC keyboard and a Szymanowski symphony that Mark gave her. She wanted to make something, create in honor of and in counterpoint to all the creations around her. A literary agent who was an old friend had just been staying at her apartment, annoying her and interrupting her time alone. He was negative about most things because, as we all know, Business is hard. She just was on the phone with a filmmaker who now said the festivals were all relationships. This director had made herself a producer, Mira remembered, because she had told Mira she had all the contacts. Business may be hard but what is needed more is patience for listening to people.

In Mira's e-mail was the film itself. The agent and she would watch it later. Everyone making things, everywhere she turned.

Just last night, she received a call from a man who was left nothing at all by his recently deceased 500-million-dollar rich father. The father left everything to a young woman and an art endowment. Nothing for the son. He wanted Mira to write a book about how his father ruined him and he wanted to make a million dollars off the book. Can she do it, he asked, in a spiritual manner?

She told the agent about the book when she got off the phone.

"What's the story?" he asked.

"Evil Zeus father," Mira said.

"Who cares?" the agent said.

Her best friend earlier had called about the bathroom renovations she was making. Now that was a Who cares? Mira said nothing as her friend ranted on. What we all do to sound important to ourselves, she thought. It's stunning.

"How is the boyfriend?" her friend suddenly asked Mira.

"The same," Mira answered obliquely. Her friend was referring to Kurt. It was odd to hear him referred to as a boyfriend.

In point of fact, Kurt had just sent Mira one of his more loving emails. Ça va? in the subject line. That was it. That was all he wrote. A man of powerful commitments.

At least if you are a musician you play with people. If you

are a filmmaker, you work with people. If you are a writer, you are alone.

Last night Mira opened a page in each of her published books to reread. She chose her age as the page number. Shockingly, all of them referred to loneliness. The film director said Mira's screenplay was about loneliness. Mira had been surprised. She hadn't known that.

Last night she had dinner with Mark. He took her to an overpriced steak house that was dangerously near Kurt's apartment. Kurt never knew where she was and she never knew where he was, except perhaps fawning over some young woman serving him food at his table.

Would she run into him there with a woman? She almost hoped so because then she could rightfully run away. But she didn't really want to leave Kurt. Time had proved that.

"I am frightened you will spend your life with him," a friend had once said to her.

"I am too," she answered.

She arrived happy at the restaurant since she loved doing a man thing with a man, not going out for the requisite female "salad."She had a bourbon. She ordered a hangar steak. In a few minutes, she thought she'd ask for a horse to ride out on.

Next to them a Japanese young couple in their early twenties ate two rounds of hors d'oeuvres, soups, and then enormous steaks, all while never saying a word to each other.

"Why do they not talk?" she asked Mark.

"The culture."

But the young girl smiled so easily and widely at her boyfriend between chews. Her perfect young face. Laughed at his occasional statement. Chew.

Mira must remember to smile like that.

Kurt always told her to smile. She imagined that if she didn't smile, she must look old, and that was what he didn't like. But maybe she was wrong. The Sufis and the Buddhists were always recommending smiling as a spiritual practice.

She knew she always ran to the worst-case interpretations with Kurt. What would happen, she asked herself, if she was not so hypersensitive? But he so casually fed her dismissive and cruel lines for her to teeter on.

The other night Kurt had asked why a certain friend of hers refused to get to know him better.

"He thinks you're a playboy," she answered.

"Well I am one," Kurt said.

"Don't say that to me," she answered.

"What is the opposite of a playboy?" he asked, now turning

into a lawyer. She dropped the subject.

After Mark and she finished their steaks, Mark went on and on about something, as those Mahlerians do, but the restaurant had become loud so she sat back, not hearing a word he was saying, and kept nodding. He was speaking with a vehemence that made her sure whatever he was saying was uninteresting.

She watched the young couple so she could learn how to smile, although watching the girl and her beautiful generous smile seemed to stun Mira instead.

Mark had told her that her career was starting now. It was all going to happen now. She had no idea what he was basing that on except the exuberance she had walked into the steak house with. That held positive portent for him.

Creativity, she thought. How sexual desire lubricates it. Young students wrote sex scenes, those scenes were part of their daily lives. Would she sit naked anymore with someone? Would anyone want her to?

It was a loss she refused to take. She just refused.

She tuned into Mark now at the restaurant. She had to admire what he said, "Children go a little far away and then come running back. Maybe you are testing out intimacy and then you run back to your bunker."

"Maybe," he said, cutting into his rib eye," I could provide some comfort to you."

"What do you mean?" she said stricken.

"Maybe I could be someone you could feel safe with. "

She looked at him, terrified.

"If I may," he said. "At the risk of sounding clichéd or sentimental."

"What?" What was he talking about and why now? Why doesn't she have another drink?

"I am saying, you idiot, that I would like that," he answered.

For the rest of the evening, she held onto those particular kind words in her psyche like smooth stones that kept her from flying away.

CHAPTER 9

"You should come to my home," Mark said, as they sat in his living room, watching the city switch on its lights in the evening.

"I am in your home."

"No, I have a house in the country. You have heard of the countryside?"

"I have," she smiled.

"No plays, no music, no friends to meet, no Strand, no taxis, no noise, no overspending in restaurants. Will you be able," he asked, "to survive?"

"Possibly," she said.

If only he knew. Or maybe he was saying he did know. She

and tranquility had never had an easy relationship.

"I can manage for a few days," she said.

He laughed. "I am not going to kidnap you."

"No?"

"Why? Do most men want to?"

She laughed. "Probably not."

He never asked her about why she was not available much. He had not asked if there was a Kurt in her life. This intrigued her. Going to the country could make Mark and her closer. It would be a first step away from Kurt or maybe it would be a step back to Kurt. She might find out she couldn't stand being with Mark three days straight. She hardly liked being with herself that long. And yet she knew, she had read, that there is something that happens with continued intimacy, the way we drive into the edges of each other, how we settle into each other's blood flow. She knew that was what happened and should happen. After all, she had been married and liked the unity of it.

She looked over at Mark suspiciously. He smiled cannily, perhaps knowing that he was offering to take her across a river, not Styx, but one she had refused herself.

"When are we going?" she asked.

"This weekend."

When she saw Kurt.

"Can we go on Sunday, Monday, Tuesday?" she replied.

He nodded slowly. She sensed he would go at her pace. He was smart enough for that. He knew, when you push, people push away.

"You choose," he said.

"Okay. I will email you when I look at my calendar."

He was reading something. "There is a Mahler board meeting next week," he added, as a distracting non sequitur.

She laughed. How we all protect ourselves.

The country incites eros, she remembered a former lover saying. She had met him in Barcelona. She had been reading Cioran in the sun, waiting for her hotel room to be ready after a transatlantic flight. He had sat down near her at the outside café she was reading in and began talking, thinking she was a student with her pen out marking up Cioran's aphorisms.

She was thrilled he knew Cioran and, she noted, he was unusually handsome with his thick curly dark hair, dark penetrating eyes, trim body. He turned out to be French, teaching Medieval Literature at Hebrew University. He was there looking at manuscripts.

They agreed to walk Barcelona together later that day. They

met at a statue and he guided them to the old Jewish cemetery on the hill, and then to the harbor. A dog came up to them and he moved away, saying, "Like all Jews, I am atavistic." She could not think what he meant. She cannot now remember his name but in the cab leaving the cemetery, on the way to dinner, he had kissed her. She had been shocked, but did not move away to protect her aloneness, as she so often did.

A writer leads a man's life at her keyboard. She was, daily, Scott going to the South Pole.

She and the atavistic French Jew went to dinner and it was clear they would stay in his room that night. She remembered they made love rather vigorously. She was comfortable with him which was interesting, given they did not know each other. Now, she had no memory of it. She left in the early morning and she did remember being out in that strange city in an area she did not know, there was early morning construction on the streets where she stood looking for a taxi to her lesser hotel. She felt desired, eternally female; she could have been anywhere getting out of a man's bed. The geography was their bodies.

That morning, she worked on her own novel, her legs up on her bed, feeling young and full.

Later he came to her hotel to find her. Again they walked,

parks, Gaudi, the church, dinner again and they talked and talked, books, observations about the Chinese family sitting next to them in the restaurant, again they made love. He told her about the shofar, it was the Jewish New Year, and what it meant. It all sounded like poetry to her. She thought she could fall in love with him. Here was a man who had a mind.

They chatted casually. Do you have siblings? How old are you?

Ah, he was twelve years younger. She had no idea, with his sad thoughtful face. He could have been an old man in ways.

He had no idea she was twelve years older. Or maybe he did.

"It's a generation," she said. At that moment, she knew there was no hope for them. He tried, without much fervor, to say twelve years wasn't that much.

Years later she found out her French Jewish lover had been living with a woman during their Barcelona affair. He had neglected to mention that along their many walks and talks.

They wrote each other for years but he never visited. It was one of those things, as they say. Was Mark one of those things? No, because she would no longer have one of those things, one of those things is boring.

Even Kurt wasn't one of those things. Kurt probably chased other women. But he had kept faithful to the relationship's endurance.

CHAPTER 10

The ocean was a deeper blue than the pale blue sweater and pale blue shorts she had been wearing that day. She had walked over to the boardwalk, pulling into her that steady crescendo and then the gentle wash sound of the water slithering back to rejoin the larger ocean. She and the young man her own age, blonde and handsome with absolutely nothing in common with her, were to meet up at the end of Long Beach.

She had developed a crush on him when her father bought live lobsters from this blonde boy of fourteen or fifteen who managed the lobster tank and smelled like brine and whose hair shone in the sun as the gold rays came in sideways through the slats in the lobster shack.

The two young people had walked on the boardwalk to a large rock at the end of the beach and climbed up onto it. Then they lay back. They must have made some conversation. But soon they were intently kissing and then he put his hand under her sweater and began fondling her breasts, over and over, insistently, because they weren't supposed to be doing that at 14, and then he kept trying to touch her down there, no, no, she kept moving his hand away, but of course her body was on wild asserted alert, augmented by the smell of the sea and the feel of the sun on them, and the horizon which was like a metaphor for what they had in front of them but somehow they knew they, as a couple, had no trajectory together, he a small town boy, she a visitor to the fishing town. So they just absorbed the sensuality of that afternoon that they both stimulated in the other.

She never ever forgot that day in light blue, and the absolute purity and eroticism of what their bodies could feel. It was drunken, the pull of giant internal waves, and it felt very much like love but wasn't, but the feeling was so good, it didn't matter.

"You are made for love," a man once told her when she had no feelings at all for him. She was in his bed, because at 22, that was what she did, got into bed with them to find out what she could of who they were, although she rarely did, but that statement itself was what was fascinating, because she felt no love at all and neither did he, but the body, the body felt like love to him.

And with Kurt, when she slept enwrapped with him, as he was very slowly learning to do, his tight skin, even though he was not young but he was athletic, and the hair on his arms and chest, felt like love to her. Is it that she was simply drawn to his naked body with his strong arms and wide shoulders and quick legs in bed, and nothing else? At the dinner party, he pontificated on death and aging to her friends, a couple who were like family to her, a couple who had been more sensitive to her at each dinner than he had been in a year. At the dinner, he did not let anyone else speak, and worse, did not make any sense.

She and the couple finally gave up trying to insert themselves into the conversation. The husband politely agreed with most of what Kurt said. One almost had no choice.

Mira was embarrassed. What she suspected was true. He was busy ranting away to young chefs every night, with his scotches and full course meals, and their comely bodies and smiles looking at him. He was drunk on their beauty and their nodding heads and the food they served him without real engagement.

He is going mad, Mira thought, in such isolation.

She remembered crossing over the gearshift in a car parked at a motel in New Hampshire when she thought the man she eventually married had cheated on her. He probably hadn't but she so loved his body that she had to ensure it, she had to be fastened to it, so she made love to him in the car right then, so he was hers. He was a little shocked. She didn't care because there was not a second to wait, not a nanosecond before she had to take away the feeling of separateness.

But that was about claiming, holding onto the body.

But there were other times when she was desirous of love simply because the man desired her. She would have an orgasm because somehow the man had made it all so erotic, had made her so erotic to herself, but after, she felt distant, betrayed by her own sexual need and narcissism. How cheap she was. Her body had given itself to him but her mind had not. She had only wanted herself at that moment, as the man had trickily conveyed her to herself. They had both made love to an image, a graven image that the man had made of her. They both were drawn to she, as a false idol.

And then the image passed.

She sat in her office listening to Pink Floyd and that song

The Great Gig in the Sky, the woman's powerful singing, which had always seemed to Mira a woman's erotic ecstasy making love, but when she read about the piece, the artists said the singing was about death.

And now she was searching for a man again who would make her feel like she did on that rock by the sea. It was not an unreasonable request. Like the man telling her about the woman who kissed him in the car. He wanted that sea rock too. Perhaps she should buy herself a blue sweater and blue shorts. What was different then from now besides her lost youth?

Her friend said you know you love the man if you can't keep your hands off him.

Kurt did not understand the rock and the sea but, to his credit, he understood that to get even close to it, you must try and create a sea rock. He understood that you build a fire in the fireplace, that you sleep together naked and you go to the sun on holidays. That is what they shared, she suddenly realized. They went to plays that he carefully chose to interest her, movies that she chose to interest him, and dinners, consistently in the sun of those events on those nights. He only touched her when he was asleep, he could be needy in his body then, but he did not touch her awake and that was why she was going to the country with

Mark -- to get on that rock.

Kurt would not claim her. His hands did not touch her body.

Would Mark's country house be that rock? It was not her experience that houses with their stolidness were those places. But she hadn't known about that sea rock till she was on it.

CHAPTER 11

That Saturday she waited for her 17-year-old student in a coffee shop. He took a bus in from the Bronx. He arrived, motioned with his hands for her to stand up so he could hug her. They did and she so loved him, this boy who had grown up with her. When he was twelve, she would say, "Let's both describe the other people sitting here but let's not be obvious. I don't want us to be arrested."

He enjoyed that. A little danger thrown in.

They would both write and then read their descriptions to each other.

Now he dropped his writing proudly on the table as he went to get a coffee at the counter. He dropped fire onto the table. She reached for it and began.

He was drunk on words, and she often had to say, "But what does that mean? It can't just sound good," but she knew only too well that seduction. She didn't say to him that men so often have just sounded good and it meant nothing.

"What do you mean by that?" she asked. That question alone might be one of the reasons men's hands no longer flew to her body.

She remembered a visit from her ex husband and his new significant other years back. Mira had felt shy, old news, with his shiny new love. Her ex pontificating nonsensically about business and his girlfriend had looked up from Mira's piano stool adoringly at her ex as he went on and on. And Mira said, the archetype all of a sudden of the ex wife, "But what do you know about business? You've never worked in a corporation."

And there, she knew, lay the difference.

But years later she and her ex had been ice-skating and he had said, "If I hadn't had those years of freedom with you, I couldn't handle the constraints of this relationship." Mira was the good guy now.

Mira had fallen that day with him on the ice and cracked her shoulder. She got up like nothing had happened and continued skating with him. After they left, it took six months for her to recover.

"When are we going to the country?" Mark asked again.

"I will tell you in 2 days when I know my schedule," she answered. She was stalling being captured. It was an old story for her.

He said nothing, then "Fine."

CHAPTER 12

Last night she had lain awake for hours thinking about friends who were dying. She would lie there and think, about death, about her being alone, then she'd bring herself to orgasm. Always to the image of Kurt and a young woman. She forgave herself for this image because she did the same when she was young. She'd masturbate to images of her husband with young beautiful women even when Mira was young and beautiful herself. Envy was an aphrodisiac for her.

Kurt's bevy of chefs always changed every five months. Then, onto the next one. But in her fantasies an imaginary one stands scantily dressed in his kitchen cooking and she has, of course, a perfect body. He is beside himself, drugged on her body.

Mira wanted to be drugged on a body or a pusher of her own body again. She was drugged a touch, she realized, on Mark's intelligence, Kurt's form, but not enough. She wants to up the substance. The drug feels like the only fight against death, she realizes, with not much originality. The body as an object of pleasure, before it becomes an object of decay. No wonder all these old men want young women.

Oddly, for her, it did not result in her wanting to be with a young man. It was her own youth she wanted. Her own undecayed body. But it couldn't come back, so only the feelings could. And how, she wondered, could she get those again?

In other words, how does a woman in her sixties fight death with sex? Sleep with anyone, a friend told her.

Mira had known women who do that. Mira had listened to women tell the most convoluted stories of men who had shown up and just slept with the women, then left them, onto other women and the stories had seemed more about loss than sex, to Mira.

Mira was a snob. She could not make love with just anyone. She enjoyed men but didn't really like their sort of myopic vision where they themselves seemed to fill up most of the screen. That type seemed to come packaged in particular brands of cellophane, which are, in fact, particular brands of defense. They could be typed into categories, a lot of them not worth unwrapping.

That was her problem.

A poet used to say to her when talking about sex, Leave your mind in your behind.

It was funny. But not possible for her, she learned.

"Mark?"

"Yes Mira." His voice was even, as if he had been expecting the call.

"Want a visit?" She felt guilty about avoiding him.

"Sure. Come over."

"It's 3 o'clock in the afternoon."

"So?"

"Aren't you at work?"

"At home."

"Oh."

"You can work here if you like," he added. Ah, already he had figured her out.

"What do you mean?"

"Bring your computer," he said. Well, he was smart enough not to say, Bring sexy underwear. Instead, bring her object of desire.

The doorman let her up to Mr. Puccini's. There were books and papers strewn all over the floor. He smiled when she walked in. So far, that was the best part. He smiled. She smiled, like a girl, shy and sure at the same time.

"Come sit here," he said. "I won't offer you a drink."

"Good."

Beethoven was playing. She was surprised. She listened.

"I am testing out this recording, whether I like the conductor."

"Do you?"

"Not really. I mean I find I am not concentrating on the music unlike, if it were perfect, I would have to. Even if you were in bed with me."

"Yes."

He looked at her slowly. She was standing, still wearing her white raincoat. "It's been so long since I've seen you. I thought you didn't have time for me," he said.

"I don't."

He smiled. "That's okay. I don't have time for you either. At least we have something in common."

She didn't ask if it was women or work that kept him occupied. She didn't ask because she didn't want to talk about her own reasons for not having time.

She went and sat down next to him, and slipped out of her coat. She touched his chest, gently. He smiled more. "Well what have you been doing?" he asked.

"Worrying."

"About what?"

"Friends dying. My not having enough work."

"But you're always working."

"Alright, not having enough money."

"With the boots you wear?"

"I'm not practical."

"I never would have known," he joked.

"Don't you worry?" she asked.

"Women always worry more than men."

"We feel more."

"I wouldn't say that. You make less."

"You think you can manage things. We know nobody can," she said.

He didn't reply.

"We're taught to manage things," he said, finally.

"Yes."

"What are you not saying?" he asked.

"I am not saying, Why don't you manage me because at the same time I would rebel right away but I could use someone to manage me."

"You'll let someone manage you when you're in love. Then it has a natural rhythm to it."

"When?"

"When."

She looked at him. Lucia had asked her a few days back, "Are you falling in lof with him?"

Mira studied Mark's face, the set of it, the seriousness of him and she liked him, she really did, but she was not falling in "lof" with him. She wished she could but she wasn't. Whatever backstory that makes you fall in love with someone wasn't in this story with Mark. She liked him.

If she had been in love with him, she would have no choice but to be with him. Everything would change, there would be evolution, happiness, as Whitehead would posit. There would be movement.

And there wasn't. There wasn't that particular movement she was looking for. It wasn't here, she realized.

CHAPTER 13

"You look nice," Mira's student said, and he took her hand under the coffee shop table. She took her hand away, but she didn't really want to. She knew he was innocent in his affection, after all she had opened worlds to him, but a teacher should not hold hands with her student. They both turned their focus to his poetry. As she began to read, she was shocked at the graphicness of the sex, but she kept a professorial expression. The writer must be watching, observing. But her heart quietly covered him, protected him.

He wanted to start a literary magazine, which was exactly what he should do, she believed. He has inherited $400, he told her. Her heart again quivered for him, this was a person, like her, who was banking on art. She was thrilled he was going that way because she knew, no matter how poor; it would be a rich life.

A woman at the hairdresser sat in the chair before Mira's turn and her voice droned on. Her boyfriend mistreats her, Mira heard her tell the hairdresser. Mira felt she might be talking about Kurt. That was what traveled through her own mind constantly, complaints, hurt, feeling slighted. This woman had the same ideas, or lack of them.

This woman made Mira abhor her own voice, the voice of a woman imprisoned by feeling powerless in love.

After she had read her student's writing that same morning, she and her student had gone to the Strand to look for books. While there, they ran into old friends of Mira. She introduced her young student. She felt such love for him, was proud of him, like the mother she never was.

Finally, she said to her friends, "We have to go to the Abacus bookstore."

One of her friends gestured toward the stacks and stacks of the Strand, "Nothing to read here, I guess."

Mira said, "Oh we've read everything here," and they laughed.

Waiting at the hairdresser, she felt like she would like to be in bed with someone, instead of rushing about. She'd like to be calling in room service, sandwiches, drinks. Lying on the covers. Watching movies. Snuggling. Occasionally making love.

"You will meet someone else," the hairdresser told her.

Mira had met Mark, but she didn't mention it. Mira didn't think of them in a relationship. They did not do normal things as a couple. She was the one who wouldn't let them do normal things. She did normal things with Kurt who was abnormal.

The prisoner and she used to go to hotel rooms and he would massage her before making love. She had never had that before. He bought gardenias for the bath. They would lie in hotel rooms and watch one movie after the other, make love, and just be together. One night he was meeting people in the bar and she came down, wearing a bustier and velvet slacks. He involuntarily put his hands on her waist as she sat down. It was a compulsion caused by her waist and his desire and it was as marvelous as one can be with a man. His big hands on her waist.

He would take her hand as they maneuvered through a restaurant together. He led, tall, in a black raincoat.

She would look at him and wonder if she loved him for his beauty or who he was.

At that time in her life she thought both their beauty was eternal. Now he was not as handsome as he used to be but he would be so to her if she still loved him. She would be if someone loved her.

Over the Beethoven that afternoon, Mark had said, "I don't understand why you see me when you're beautiful and brilliant."

Whom was he talking about?

Right now, while she was at the hairdresser, Mark was having friends over. She had no desire to be there. She had a desire for him to be happy. She wished the same for Kurt, who must now have returned from playing tennis and was resting.

Kurt had sent a first-time email to her during the week. "Should we go away for Christmas?"

"Yes," she answered and apparently he had arranged a surprise trip. She was sure it was Palm Beach where they had gone together before and both enjoyed.

Was there hope he would come closer?

She so needed, she felt, to walk and talk, extemporaneously, with a man. Just being together for five days would allow for that.

He was not usually emotionally or physically available to her in New York where they lived. When they met for their dinners, he would joke, evade. In New York, they had their dates, which were wonderful because she loved the cleverness of the obfuscation but, almost never in conversation, would he show vulnerability. They were like two spies out on a date. She would venture forth her feelings or needs now and then but he swatted them away quickly. It would be months before she tried again.

With other men, just being together was the date.

She had bought a bikini yesterday for her trip with Kurt, which was in a week. She looked ghastly in the lingerie store mirror. A man who knew her when she was 23 had sent her a Christmas card. This was the first she has heard from him in over 40 years.

It turned out he had followed her life, as people do now. Because of the way she looked in a bikini then. He must be old now too.

She no longer had a bustier . . . she wore them often then. Could she even wear any of that now without looking ridiculous?

A woman had told Mira to get rid of all her books, a woman from California, naturally. Her books were making her old, the woman said to Mira's amazement, but it was true that when Mira was young she did not seem to have as many books but that was because she sold them when she moved and she moved often. Now she had been in the same apartment for over 20 years. It was not the books that needed selling, it was the shifting into a new life that she needed. Perhaps she would sell what she did not want, as a start.

Maybe this bizarre statement by this woman had tiny merit.

The books were indeed sealing in her aloneness. She must do new things, the woman said, if she wanted different results.

That part was true. But Mira didn't see the books as the problem, just her attachment to the repetition, the prison yard of her mind.

That Saturday night, Kurt was late for the movie they were going to. She looked at her watch, she reapplied lipstick, she checked her phone. The airport-like crowd of moviegoers had already been troughed into the theater.

Finally, he sauntered into the empty theater lobby. "We're too late. I don't think we're going to get a seat," she said, in a clipped voice, suddenly turning into her mother.

"I had a call from a client," he replied.

"On a Saturday night?" She didn't believe him. "Who? Celine? Lucille?"

"No, Lolita."

You're not kidding, she thought. She was annoyed. The movie theater was packed and they could not sit together or even in a decent seat and she said, "We'll have to split up to see the movie," and he said, "Let's just leave. I don't need this stress from you. The movie is not that important."

So she followed his angry body out.

"Let's get money back on the tickets," he said.

"I bought them online. I don't think we can. Let's just forget it."

He raced off to the ticket booth and he stood in line in the cold and he did get the money back. "See how you're wrong about everything?" he said, as he proudly handed her twenty-three dollars.

They decided to walk to Spring Street and find a restaurant. They found a lovely bistro and he got a romantic table and they ended up having a congenial time.

"See? It all worked out," he said.

She laughed, feeling love for him, a waterfall that seemed to never stop flowing, even with her frightened mind.

After dinner they went home.

In his bedroom, he handed her the TV remote. She switched the TV on and surfed. He went off to his bathroom. She undressed when he was not in the room and got under the covers. She cursorily looked at herself in his floor to ceiling mirror. It was always disappointing.

He returned and she snuggled into him. They watched something that neither of them were that interested in just to relax. She kissed the side of his face.

His arm was around her but that would be all the tenderness from him. It would be she who made love to him. Tonight she selected a blowjob, from her repertoire. Because she lost her temper with him? Perhaps.

Chris Rock in a stand-up routine said, Never make a major decision after a blowjob.

She took some kind of cold comfort in the loneliness after, of not having been touched. She held her own breast as she lay on her side.

She thought about bodies again. Being seven maybe and she and a school friend naked in bed, touching each other's and their own bodies. Not knowing you weren't supposed to do that. The wondrousness of their bodies. Laughing at all the feelings it could bring about.

She smiled in the dark. Two little girls, like silverfish in the basement. As had been true with so many men, she couldn't remember the name of that little girl.

Her student wrote a poem about streetwalkers whom he saw on the subway and he imagined them as being and feeling nameless, even to themselves. He had a compulsion to call his name out loud on the subway car, Know my name, his poem said. My name is Senegal. Remember my name.

It was Mira's favorite of his poems. He didn't understand why but that was because he was too young to know how one's name can be lost, or eventually will be, as we street walk through life, yet he intuited, he intuited. Mira was not sure he knew what his poem was about but that didn't matter. Artists move from word to word into truth, sometimes unintentionally. Maybe more than sometimes.

She had not called Mark in three weeks. She had not made an arrangement to see him.

She had breakfast with a friend at an upscale breakfast place that was almost dizzying in how crowded it was. They remarked on how long they'd known each other.

"Yes, it's true we're old. We're lucky," Mira said, "that we're healthy. But I lie awake, thinking how does one be this age?"

"I worry too," her friend said.

"About what part?"

"Health and money."

"But you can live with your boyfriend," Mira said. "You have a normal loving kind boyfriend. I could never live with Kurt."

"It's true," she said, "we are looking for a 2 bedroom apartment together."

"Oh," Mira said, hurt. Another person going forward while she moved nowhere.

"Maybe Kurt would pay your rent," Mira's friend said.

"I guess I'll go somewhere cheap," Mira said. Although the only place she wanted to move toward was love.

Or she was waiting for a ship to come in. But if that was true, she realized, she would be sailing many ships right now. Not having breakfast with a friend at some over-expensive crowded pink and white restaurant. She would become a sea captain, navigating, pushing toward her treasure. Why didn't she do more of that?

Her emails were full of rejections of every kind.

Kurt had told her the last time he wrote her that he had a good year. She sure as hell hadn't.

In another email, he had told her his son just signed a 3 million dollar deal. Mira complimented how they both had accomplished much, as if she was complimenting the learning of a rare language.

"Kurt is always doing well," Mira said, distracted.

Her friend put her coffee down and looked directly at Mira. "You know I don't like Kurt. He thinks of no one but himself. You should meet a loving guy, like I have."

Sure, sure, Mira thought.

As she returned from shopping and breakfast, she continued reading a novel about Blacks in the South in the 30s coming up to work in Northern steel mills and the horrible events that ensued. As she read, her charge account at Bergdorf seemed like quite the ridiculous problem. Thank god she had the books that that California woman wanted her to get rid of. They taught her about proportion.

Her literary heroines pulled rabbits out of a hat late in life. Their lives were hard: usually weak men and financial difficulties. In the end, their talent saves them.

Oh please.

She did not know what else to do. She seemed to be too old to get a job in advertising or even to work in someone's office. She had been out of the mainstream so long that no one would take her seriously. She never factored in old age and how people don't want to hire someone older than themselves. Who wants their mother around that much? She had thought she could work eternally. That nothing would change.

Maybe she thought she would be saved. By what, did she think, she would be saved?

The unexpected miracle.

Art is the unexpected miracle in itself.

She must be a prizefighter, she thought, and get back up off the mat. Like those gladiators in the ring. Take all the punches, as many as she could because that was life, till she died. Go out fighting.

Well, that had been decided upon.

At another breakfast, Sally told Mira how she didn't like men.

"Why?" asked Mira.

"They forced themselves so much on me when I was young. I really hoped to be gay."

Mira listened.

"Didn't that happen to you?" her friend asked.

"It happens to all young women," Mira answered.

Mira didn't say she felt the opposite that she wanted to revive that time where men forced themselves on her. That time of urgency and desire. She knew it was the blood flow to sustaining and giving the punches.

When she ate less, Mira felt more sexual. The thinner she was, the more hungry. But her age group conspired against this. Let's meet for breakfast lunch dinner. Here, eat this. Mira could live on booze and popcorn and fruit. When she was lean, her body leaned toward the Other. It needed the bulk of another.

After breakfast, she and her friend had walked out onto the street. Her friend, who had just told her she didn't like men, has a very rich husband and was wearing a soft fur coat. Mira put her hand on it. "We should get body suits made of this," Mira said, laughing.

"Why?" asked her friend.

"It is so soft."

"You mean it would protect us?" her friend asked.

"Nothing can protect us. I just meant the softness feels so good. The fur," Mira said, touching it once again, "is so soft."

CHAPTER 14

"You don't mind that we're sitting in different rows on the plane, do you?" Kurt asked with a touch of amusement in his voice.

They were riding in the car that he had ordered for them, on the way to the airport. "I've booked us into all the restaurants down there," he said. "Only first class. And the hotel is fantastic. Only the best for you, honey. But I couldn't get us seats together on the plane."

She knew he liked extra legroom. Perhaps that was what happened.

"It's fine," she said, because, in actual fact, it was. She liked to sit alone. She was not sure he really could not get seats together or he just preferred it that way. But it didn't really matter.

As they sat together at the gate waiting for their plane to Palm Beach (she had been right), they talked about her film. He liked discussing her creative ventures. He thought he was helpful in bringing a business sense to her.

"The director doesn't care about your words," he said.

She nodded. He was right about that and it was still galling her.

"She cares about pictures. Your writing is incidental," he added.

"So acute," she said, "given you never spoke to her."

"I did a couple of times at those parties where you were all raising money," he said. "She flirted too much with me. She was after my money."

Mira said nothing. It was probably true.

"Anyway, of course I know what is going on," he said. "I'm an analyst."

It had taken years for her to know he was not joking when he said that. He truly felt his analytical skills on Wall Street were analytical everywhere else.

Once they boarded, she settled into her seat five rows behind him on the other aisle and began reading the New York Review of Books. She might even pull her computer out and go over some writing. She, like he, was always completely absorbed in something.

From her seat she could see the side of his strong face and

crinkly grey hair, as he read some paper. He could not see her. She felt such affection for him as she studied him. She found him beautiful. Masculine, elegant.

She turned back to the article she was reading about a writer and she noted that he died at 75, only five years older than Kurt, and she felt such loss, as if that would happen to Kurt.

Stop it, she thought, he has long genes and is exceptionally healthy.

"What has that got to do with it?" she could hear Lucia ask her.

Kurt would not tell Mira where they were staying in Palm Beach. It was a surprise. And then the cab pulled up to a beautiful Spanish-looking hotel with pools and cabanas. They were checked into a penthouse room, with their own private balcony and garden and a huge bed in the room. The hotel was a series of courtyards, with hundreds of different flowers and plantings.

Once they settled in, they went down to the restaurant, which was quiet and did not have the manic insistence of a New York restaurant. They discussed the news since Kurt hated any kind of personal discussion. They never sat around discussing themselves as a couple, he would never allow that, and she had adjusted to it. She, like him, maybe also felt sitting around telling each other how much you love each other or how you are misunderstanding each other can get pretty boring. Instead they were the types who preferred to show it through consistency, not picking arguments, being amenable. She told herself that they understood each other in that way.

But she was not sure. Maybe that was all rationalization for missing tender words.

In the morning they woke up and he turned on the TV only for them to see another black kid shot by a policeman but this time the kid had pointed a gun at the policeman. She felt vaguely sick as she watched the television. It seemed that time was going backwards. Kurt washed and she would take a bath later so off they went to breakfast and spoke of the disaster of it all and then walked to the pool to see what it was like and they read in their separate chairs poolside and then he wanted to walk to get some scotch for the evenings before dinner. A cocktail in the room. Off they went, past the enormous houses and their Spanish gated and flowering lawns of bougainvillea and he said, "This is the playground of the rich."

She thought yes, I could live here. I, who live on the edge. For some reason she felt rich, especially walking in all this beauty. It didn't take much for her to feel rich, the sun, music, perfume, a walk like this, a man she loved.

"I'm going to play tennis in a half hour," he said. "With the pro, Roxanne," and he gave her a provocative smile to get a rise out of her.

Business as usual, she thought. Chefs, female tennis pros. As he went off with his bag, she went to the lobby to answer emails, for that was where the wireless was. Something in her knew he would flirt with the female tennis pro but she still sat there happy, feeling, dared she even feel it, loved. He liked his privacy and his aloneness, yet he was with her here, by the sea, the place she felt the most herself.

Earlier when they had gone to buy sunblock and whiskey for him, just that walk together felt sustaining. She felt like he was her husband, at least in her heart and isn't that where a husband should reside? Sometimes they walked in silence, and she felt the gentle tenderness in that silence.

After she had finished with the wireless in the lobby, she returned to their private balcony and wrote. Tennis usually took 2 hours, so she still had some time for herself. She loved the sun on her and the quiet. She was sure that if she could choose the idyllic life, it would be being alone writing in the sun with the water nearby, and then in the night having a husband she loved come home to her. This was what she wanted. But he was not, however, the least attracted to that. He loved the distractions of New York and the intellectual fascinations there, theater and working, and he loved being free.

She was surprised, on their holiday, that he did not want a car, did not want to explore the area. He just wanted to be by the beach, play tennis, and read. Sort of like her, sans the tennis. At night they walked to the small town to the various indoor and outdoor restaurants.

As she told Lucia later, "It was lovely. Really lovely."

And then Mira fell silent. Because it wasn't that she and Kurt had got any closer. He held himself, as always, eyes closed in bed, separate.

"Well," Lucia said, "was he passionate?"

"Kurt?" Mira laughed.

"Who else?" Lucia said.

"It felt," Mira hesitated and then,"like warm water that never gets hot."

CHAPTER 15

"What do you mean by warm water that never gets hot?" Lucia asked as they sat in her apartment the next day, some type of classical dance music playing in the background. Mira had brought in coffees. "Are you speaking sexually?"

Mira noted that Lucia's voice was not the voice of an octogenarian but of a young girl.

"Oh," Mira answered. "Sex is all his genitals, like a baby." She smiled. "I must feel there is some purity in service."

"You are as crazy as he is," Lucia answered. Again the clipped Austrian accent.

"No doubt."

And thus her sexual connection to Kurt did not take place in her own genitals, but in the oddest of places. Mira sat back and remembered when they were in bed in their cozy beautiful room in Palm Beach and an unrelenting Florida rainstorm with thunder rolled into the night. The rain was beating hard on the Spanish tiled roofs. She woke up and there he was, naked, slinking around the room in the dark, not knowing she was watching him, carefully checking the windows to be sure the water was not coming in. He moved her phone away from the open window and shut one of them.

"There was something about that which is sexual," she said to Lucia. "He was tending. Yes, yes, I am left alone physically by him, but I loved those actions. I am frightened, Lucia, that may be what I want."

Lucia listened, trying to understand.

"I spend so much time," Mira continued, "ruing that I am not young and beautiful because I feel that would provide the sexual energy we are missing for him to want to really be with me. I know that beauty spurs action in a man and I feel this is the missing ingredient to us. But I could be wrong. He may not desire a woman, only desire safety. And, Lucia, what if I am desiring the same?"

"When you meet someone you love, you won't want safety.

You'll want him."

"I hope so. But for now, I've loved safety."

Lucia pointedly said nothing, which Mira took as tacit agreement although she was not sure what Lucia was agreeing to.

"But then I also learned any beauty might do for me too," Mira said, "because when I was there I thought what if I lived in Palm Beach, by the sea and palm trees and the blue, and the gentle streets and worked in a hotel, poor, and taught if I could for extra money, and that would be it . . . Would it be a terrible life? No . . . and that tells me I do not mind being alone, if there is beauty for me to make love to. Anyway, you too, you are alone," Mira said.

Lucia said, "My husband was a very difficult man. But even so, I would have liked to remarry after he died but no one suitable presented himself."

Then Lucia turned to Mira. "You have to understand, my dear girl, that not everyone lets themselves be overcome."

Which led Mira to remembering something else about the trip. She and Kurt had been sitting outside having dinner on Christmas Eve at an outdoor restaurant in Palm Beach, festive, all lit up for Christmas with lights and lanterns. And there was a table of people next to them and a Chinese woman who looked ancient, maybe she was 80, Kurt thought she was 100, and seated next to that woman was a man in his 60s, with dyed floppy hair, who kept looking over at Mira, in embarrassment. The Chinese woman looked rich and the man looked poor and she must have been keeping him.

Kurt said, "That is your fiction mind thinking that up," but Mira was sure she was right. What does that man think about, she wondered, when he makes love to her ancient face?

"He looks drugged," Kurt responded.

Lucia and Mira sat quietly for a bit. "Have you heard from Mark?" she asked.

"Yes. He emails me."

"What will you do?" she asked.

"I don't know. I am loyal in my way."

CHAPTER 16

One evening on their trip Kurt found a place for them to have dinner, a grille restaurant with live jazz. He had seen it walking back from tennis. When they arrived that night, she loved the casualness of it, a dark, open restaurant with space between the tables and chairs and none of the prissiness of the more expensive places. Her drink, when it came, was big, and she sort of delighted in the way Kurt looked dashing in a handsome shirt and jacket, and she knew, even though she couldn't see them at this particular moment, he was wearing, as usual, tight pants. Who thought she would fall for a metrosexual? Did that make her one?

They shared a surf and turf and two salads for dinner. They

were gay, trying to figure out the plethora of what looked like limousine drivers and their wives, who allegedly came every Friday night to dance. The crowd seemed locals and older than she and Kurt, but they probably weren't. Fat, ungainly men in black shirts and white ties or men in red shirts with dyed hair, turned out to be lithe and swan-like when these men and their women, in mu mu dresses and big costume jewelry, got out on the dance floor. The music suffused a driving rhythm into the room. Kurt returned from the men's room and offered her his hand to dance.

"Those shoes are not your best dancing shoes," he said, when her high-heeled sandals flopped across the floor as she moved.

She agreed.

When a Motown song came on next, they both wanted to dance, so she went up to the dance floor barefoot. He said, "I'm the lead." And he, who did not like to touch, grabbed her firmly and had his hand strongly on the small of her back.

The bartender sang a Frank Sinatra song not particularly badly or well and she asked Kurt, "Can you sing, too?"

He nodded. She laughed to herself, he probably could.

As they walked home in the warm Florida night on wealthy quiet avenues with majestic houses with Spanish type iron gates and hedges and flowers everywhere, and a moon in the sky and the sea nearby, they held hands and she said, "I could live here if I were with you."

"You'd last two weeks, without Lincoln Center and theater, and your thousand friends, and . . ."

Let me push you away.

"I'd be happy with you," she replied honestly, like a little girl. She realized she had never been this committed before and was it just that she was older and more able to, less bedeviled by a frantic need for independence, or was it just that he was right for her?

Her husband, in the end, had wanted a housewife and mother in one. The prisoner had ended up wanting a golf partner and someone to cook for him. Others simply hadn't wanted anyone.

When they got home, they went to bed and she put on a TV show about a song writer in the 40s, 50s and 60s and together they silently watched the big bands and the real Frank and Jack Jones and Nancy Wilson and she snuggled up to him and soon began playing with his body, and then she turned off the sound on the TV in the middle of the show and she got on top of him as always. He shut his eyes, is it because her breasts have fallen and she has a bit of a stomach, he never says I am happy with you or you are what I want or anything romantic, he simply uses a line from one of her characters in a book of hers he had read, "I'm here aren't I?" on those rare times she asks for reassurance.

He knew it was her husband who used to say that when she asked if he loved her.

Her husband too was loyal, steadfast and rarely verbal in his love. Lucia had once posited that Mira was the type of woman who distrusted superlatives and thus chose men mute in love. Maybe Lucia was right. Those men who shower you with compliments, you know it's because they want to hear them back.

Of course, she often showered Kurt with compliments. "I take that as a compliment," he would say. And, in his way, he did say sweet things to her. "You're kind and loving," "I love you like I love my mother and I love my son." Compliments she refused to cotton to. They seemed old fashioned and distant in themselves.

After he came, they lay down and finished watching the show. The last few shots were of the songwriter marrying late in life and, then, they said he died at 77. Seven years older than Kurt.

She touched his body as a way of saying goodnight and then she turned on her side in grief.

CHAPTER 17

On the flight back, she and Kurt were seated together. When they discovered there was a free seat in their row, they decided to put the open seat between them. She would have preferred being next to his body. She had always got up close to her husband on a plane, another body she had loved passionately. Now her husband was with another woman but whenever Mira saw her ex husband, Mira often found her hands going to his body and she had to pull them back. And here she had chosen, for Kurt's love of privacy or was it hers; after all she was going to be on her computer, she had chosen that the seat between them stay empty. Convenience over passion. Was this their age?

Being on the plane reminded her of a flight she had been on, in her late twenties, it was before her husband was in her life and he came in when she was thirty, and just remembering he had come into her life at all reminded her how much she was a woman who had been lucky in love, always with someone, and still now in her 60s, dating and being with a man who inspired her, bringing her joy and beauty, dinners, films, drinks on his terrace and by the fire. Who took her away. Who gave her expensive scarves she did not need (only to find out later they were strangely his mother's) and she bought him shirts he did not need.

Of course, as with all love, he disappointed her. Angered and brought her loneliness. If you love them, Adam Phillips writes, they become a problem to you.

She was remembering she had sat next to a very handsome young man of her own age on a plane before she met her husband and under the blankets hands were flying over each other everywhere. The urgency of the body. They must have both had orgasms.

They never saw each other again.

How her body ached to be touched. This, this she had forsaken with Kurt, as well as the possibility for cohabitation and marriage. Those were the price tags for his body. Another man would touch her, they always had before. But she had now, to mix up the words of Leonard Cohen, decided to have her perfect body touched by her own mind.

Autoeroticism.

This afternoon, when they land, Mira will leave Kurt with the knowledge that some new young eager girl would move into his apartment, the last one's visa having expired, and this new one would share a life with him as his chef. He told her just this morning as they had breakfast overlooking the hotel fountain, sitting outside in the Florida sun, that just last night he had dreamed about his new chef's arrival. "She was a bit heavier," he said, "than I thought she would be but not too heavy."

She did not respond. What was he trying to tell himself?

Mira too had had dreams, but hers were about needing money and, just when things were getting most difficult for her (in her dream), checks came in the mail with sewing assignments. Mira interpreted this dream to mean she lived on a thread. Some stitch came in just when it was needed. A good omen and then, when she got home in reality, after their trip together, she found that friends had sent her checks. For threading. But was she worthy of this generosity?

Those patrons of Beethoven and Rilke, they were funding historically important work. Could she deliver that to her own patrons? Did Rilke and Beethoven ever write terrible work? Balzac wrote 22 novels, only 11 of which were published. It's difficult for all of us, she thought.

Mark had been busy with friends over the holidays but, even away with Kurt, they had exchanged emails. She felt they were a lifeline to him and maybe they did siphon off some of her own need for dialogue from Kurt. He wrote he was scared. Of what, she wondered. Mark had written her a plaintive note that he felt sad after all these Xmas celebrations and he looked forward to those private moments of responding to her notes.

But for her to switch romantic horses, he would have to so outdo Kurt and that seemed unlikely. Six years was a long time to be enthralled with someone. Kurt didn't have many friends but he had one whom he had gone to college with, Marty.

When she met Marty, he had surprised her by saying, "You two have lasted. You seem to be able to put up with his quirks."

She nodded.

"Do you see other men?" the friend asked.

She was shocked.

Exuberance, Kurt had said, when she asked about why he lived with the last woman. The woman was 26 years younger and in love with him so we can assume it was sex. That woman left him for a young man, probably also sex, her own need to be touched, and that did not last either. Kurt's 23 year younger wife also left him for another man with whom it did not last.

"I am protecting us," he said, when Mira asked why he chose not to live with her. "We won't split up this way. All your relationships break up," he said.

"But people change," she answered. "We grow up."

"I am protecting us," he said again and ended the conversation.

She had told him a friend had tamed raccoons. "I thought they were wild," she said to Kurt. "Untamable."

"You mean like you?" he said.

When he met her, he had said, "You don't seem the type to marry."

Which one of them was he talking about?

The last night in their hotel room, when they made love she was annoyed with him. He had said something hurtful which she now forgot and she was on top of him as always and he of course was not touching her – those self help books in the bookstore had said he does not love you if he does not touch you – but somehow she stopped thinking about that as he was inside her and, for one of the many few times, she thought about herself and she almost could have had an orgasm. She was building towards it but then he finished.

As she lay awake in the night, she wondered what she would do if a man said to her, "I want you to have an orgasm." She was frightened she was no longer able to.

CHAPTER 18

When they returned to New York, Mira moved in with a friend who was ill. Her friend had a beautiful apartment with large windows that looked over a sculpture garden and Mira had her own room and her own bathroom. This more elegant part of the city was quieter than Mira's bohemian area and the trendy area where Kurt lived. It was a place with a large gracious lobby, in other words, of wealth, and there was a strange counterpoint to it all for her. She was still not making ends meet and she needed to think about it, but her heels tapped along marble walkways and to dining tables with tall standing silver candelabras. Friends sent her money, Kurt took her to a fancy holiday and now she was staying with another friend who had a 5-star apartment. Why did wealth surround her like this but not come close to her?

Was it because she chose art as a life, and she had enough success to be published or produced but not enough to make a living, and her friends so beautifully rallied around to support her in this? But that is no way to live so she decided to look for work, any work at all, but what she wanted was to write for someone. Her only happiness work wise was when her fingers and mind, like a pianist, were in engagement and making beauty out of something, all the everyday stories where we search so diligently for our own and others' truths. It was always there, if one opened the heart. Those stories were a fervor for her, a sexual fervor. One she depended on.

She met friends for meals in expensive hotels. She herself wore expensive boots. Money had never been real to her. Money was energy, an older student had said, who apparently had no money now, after a life of making millions. But people's versions of having no money always differed.

This student was a beautiful woman with dark hair, sharp dark eyes, slender, and a face-lift that said she had had a face-lift. She was also smart, and canny. Hard to believe this woman would have the dreamer, self destructive side that Mira had, one of banking on art and men who wanted to be left alone. Her student sat in Mira's apartment in designer clothes, lavish jewelry and fur wraps. But Mira did not envy this woman's material items. She had always known we come in with little and leave with even less. Mira's prize possession had been her mind and it used to be her beauty because it helped her and this was why she was sad at her beauty forsaking her, if it was.

Years ago, an agent told her to write a love story. Never would she think that the most difficult of all her love affairs would end up being a love story. That her vulnerability, willingness to love a man who would not open his heart would become a journey, one she could not abort at will. She was learning this time about staying, about not being ambivalent. His weaknesses were his. Her passions were hers.

In bed one night, she had asked, "Do you think we'll always be together?"

"Yes," he answered.

"Do you think you'll be happy?"

"Yes," he said and then turned away.

She woke to a note from Mark telling her that it was time for her to come to the country and that it was his plan to make her wish she never had to leave. It was his plan to make her life easier, if he did not do that, he was worth nothing. She was not sure what to make of such an open hand. It made her realize the many things Kurt did not say to her.

Lucia said, "Finally a man with some sense. Kurt is not your end."

Mira looked a bit dejected.

Lucia said, "It is best for you to be with someone who can give, make a life. This is what normal men do."

Mira stood up and sat down, not even noticing she was doing that.

"Are you going to his country house?"

"Yes," Mira said. "I am forcing myself to."

"Why? What is so wrong with him?" Lucia asked.

"I don't know. But I sense something . . . or I would have gone towards him, wouldn't I?"

Lucia didn't answer and went back to her newspaper.

Finally, Mira heard, "With someone else that might be true. I am not so sure about you."

CHAPTER 19

At dinner last night Mira had fixed up one of her student's with Kurt's son for a small party she gave for Kurt's birthday. His son lived in Washington and his father had guided him to becoming as successful as he was. His son flipped real estate properties, his father having helped him launch, and now he had a large portfolio. Kurt admired, even created, his son's work ethic and they talked business incessantly.

Both men had handsome faces, with their intent quick dark eyes.

Her student, Gemma, had been coming to her for a long time to work on Gemma's book. Mira taught in her living room and would sit there in her bare feet and discuss the trajectory of characters and language. Mira had an outlier business doing this, working outside the university system, having been too lost when young to know how to intelligently craft a future. Then it was not men she was nihilistic about, it was herself.

Gemma was to be the son's date at Kurt's birthday dinner, since Gemma had complained of not meeting a good man. She had a perfect body, one toned from hours at the gym, and she was smart, original, and had long blonde hair and sultry blue eyes. When Mira entered the restaurant, Kurt was already there, standing over Gemma who was seated at the bar, as they waited for a table. Kurt could not take his eyes off her. When the evening was over, Mira was surprised that the son did not offer to walk Gemma home. After she left, Kurt told his son how hot she was. "And she has a colossal figure," he said.

The son agreed that Gemma was beautiful but did not explain his not pursuing her. Later Mira found out that the son had told Gemma that his father insisted he shave off his beard to come to dinner.

Gemma had said, "Why did you listen? Beards are great."

The son must not have liked being seen as under his father's rule. Kill the messenger.

Mira felt angry that Kurt was so taken with Gemma's body

but understood the statements were true.

"I like your dress," Kurt said to Mira in the morning. "Check your gloves as you leave," he said.

She found out later he had put money in her gloves for the birthday dinner she'd paid for last night.

Kurt told her another chef was moving in with him tomorrow. She could hear in the background the singer, Kem's, vocal Intimacy on the stereo, a soft crooning voice promising a woman everything. This chef is from Luxembourg but is Greek and educated in England, he said. He sounded excited.

Exuberance, he said, when she asked what the other women had whom he had lived with. She was sure he meant sexual desire, his and theirs.

Kurt's chefs are an addiction, a friend told Mira.
And here Mira was getting addicted to his unavailability to her.
He wasn't the one who had to go cold turkey. She did.

What were her addictive sexual times, like he'd had with all the young women in his past? When she was a young woman, she too had made love on the couch, on the floor, up against the walls. She'd worn tight pants and tops that stopped under her breasts. Sometimes she wore a black evening dress that went to the ground because she thought it made her look thinner. She wore hot pants. She wore dresses with buttons down the front that snapped open. She never wore a bra. One time she went out dancing in a see through blue gauze dress. All for her reign of sexual power and wanting people to be addicted to her. She was much younger than her lover who kept a life size nude photo of her up on his wall.

And then that exuberance changed to an exuberance of a different kind.

She began loving repressed intelligent men. Who were not that good in bed, not that affectionate, not that romantic. But she liked their wit and the twists of their minds. They were more likely addicted, not to sex, but to booze or to talking. She loved what they said, rather than how they touched her. She would sleep over in their imaginatively constructed and furnished homes, full of paintings and ocean views, and walk home in the mornings wearing the man's hat.

Then she had a purely sexual affair, where the painter would slip into her bed in the morning at 4 a.m. She loved the strangeness of it, or was it the isolation? He had a perfect body and she seemed to think she did then too. She ate less at night to be prepared for her morning visitor. Maybe she went to bed earlier.

Then there was her husband. He was sensitive but maybe not repressed. They had sex all the time. He was rough and masculine, and like Kurt, beautifully built. She could not leave him, even though they fought all the time. His body held her. She desired his earthiness. She liked that he objectified her. Turn around. He preferred her back to him.

She could not leave him.

But in the end, they wanted different lifestyles, he by the sea and with a family, and she thinking she wanted to be in the city and live a life of unlimited options.

After it ended, she had her first affair where she responded to the man, how he felt, how he touched her. It was the prisoner when he got out. He began rebuilding his life, as a building contractor for himself, it was all he could get and became a success within a few years. He loved her and taught her what it was like to be loved and be taken care of. Her husband had been self-conscious. The prisoner liked to play the romantic lead in a woman's life. He had learned how to make love to a woman, in and out of bed. But she had not been able to say yes to forever with him. And so she went off again to her imaginary unlimited options. But he had made it easier for her to respond to the next man. The good lover, it seemed, unlocked something.

But, after the next bad lover, she closed down again.

Then Kurt. Kurt, in the repressed intelligent category.

A friend of hers, Alan, a male analyst, said, "But how can you get turned on if he does not kiss you?"

She couldn't. When Alan said that to her, she forgave herself for being cold.

Alan said, "You don't even think about Mark."

"No," she said.

"It's you who want to be alone."

"No I don't."

"Face it, honey, Kurt gives you the space for your creative mind. That's your attachment."

CHAPTER 20

She had been working all day and into the night. She was to go to Kurt's after finishing and she was excited about relaxing with him next to his fireplace, decompressing from the day. The doorman kept saying yes yes to him when they called up to him to tell him she was there. They put the phone down, a bit confused themselves.

"What did he say?" she asked.

"He asked if Natasha is coming too."

There was no Natasha. It was an imaginary name he made up. In this way, he helps her to feel she is not enough. The elevator took her up and she decided to swallow that hurt and walked down the hall and he opened the door and she immediately saw and heard two young women sitting by the fire, seductive music in the background. "It's not what it looks like," he said. "I have done nothing wrong," he added, since he knew her well enough to know two young women on his couch would immediately raise her antennae.

"It's my new chef and her friend who has come to help settle her in."

First Mira was angry. Why didn't he send them downstairs to the chef's apartment if she is coming over? But he was too polite to them for that. She knew that she was wrong to feel so furious, she should be embracing, but she was not. Why were they with him on her date with him? Why are other women always in his house?

"Why, why do I have to deal with them?" she asked him in the dining room, as she tried to corral herself. The two women were chatting in the living room and could not hear her.

"You are borderline," he said. "Go home if you can't take it because I cannot risk losing these two young women, Gaby is going to cook for me and the other one will refer me new chefs when this one leaves. The other one is a chef, too."

She told herself, Shape up. He has a right to his life. She felt he hid things from her and that already had her on edge. There was no safety for her, here.

He will hurt her. He was hurting her.

She stood there in his blue dining room with the windows overlooking the city and struggled to contain her feelings. She didn't want to run. She had done that so many times in her life when in love. Run and it had been a mistake. From her husband, the prisoner, she didn't want to run now. She knew that a relationship only lasts if you stay, work through it.

She decided to join them all in the next room, just to see if she could save the situation, if she could take the high road, not the angry and petulant road of leaving in a huff. She sat down by the fireplace and tried to be pleasant, dragged it out of her tired body, she had worked a 13-hour day, and he told the young women stories and stared at one of the young women's body, her face, and Mira thought this is so wrong.

One woman told Mira she was from Canada.

The other one had had a good flight here.

Yes, she loved her suite downstairs.

She was looking forward, she said, to getting to know New York.

As Mira politely asked banal questions, Kurt said, "Mira is probing," which also struck Mira as odd as she made the effort, against her will, to converse with them by the fire.

The two girls continued smiling and Kurt studied them and

Mira knew they felt sorry for her elderly female self.

Kurt said to them, "I am an alien doing research on earth women." They laughed on cue, as Mira had seen other chefs do to the same statement.

She really should walk out of his life, she thought. This is so stupid.

But she didn't.

Later she and Kurt decided to go to bed and leave them by the fire. When they got downstairs, he said, "You really are crazy," and she did not respond since she was busy thinking, I'll go now, and then he said,

"But you are wonderful in so many ways, Mira. I do love you."

He was hedging his bets.

He tried to get her to hold him in bed, to make love to him. She told herself to give, give, and she tried but really she was the one who needed to be held. He had no idea of that. She was sure he told himself that she was the one who was difficult. She should be able to accept anything he does. What business is his life of hers?

He was confident that she would love him, no matter what. He believed no one else would love her which was not true but it had been true heretofore that she refused to love anyone else. She was now finally of all terrible times a woman who bonded. She should be proud of that. That finally she was willing. She no longer lived looking for an escape clause. Like he seemingly did.

"I love you," he said once again, "but I am not in love with you."

"Why?" she asked.

"You know."

But she didn't know. She assumed it was her age. Maybe it was her poverty. Who the hell knew?

"I love to hear you speak," he told her. Another lover once had told her that, too. Another man who could be cruel at times and she had thought she loved him. She was going to have to change this.

Needing love can't be turned into a masochistic activity, she thought.

She remembered her first lover telling her that he was just out of a marriage and could not commit to one woman and, one day, as the other woman stood in his living room, Mira said, "I can't do this anymore." And she walked out of his apartment. She wasn't angry. He had been sweet and loving to her. She understood he wasn't ready for monogamy after years of marriage. She didn't even remember being sad because it was unequivocal for her. She'd had enough. She didn't want to be hurt. She knew then, it seemed, how to protect herself.

She had had other suitors at the time but none she particularly cared about.

Suddenly one day that same man, who could not commit, came out of the blue, looking for her on the street, visibly upset. His voice shook. She was confused when she saw him. What was he doing outside like this, not in his office, on a weekday, hovering over her like a wild bird?

He was nervous. "I'm looking for you. I cannot live without you," he said.

She was young and he had been her boyfriend and she had thought she loved him.

They did end up living together for five years. She eventually left him because he was much older, and his mind did not interest her. She was ready for her own life. Her own life was very different than his. He was settled. She was just beginning, as Kurt's chefs were.

CHAPTER 21

The next night, in her grief over Kurt and his carelessness of her, she lay in her own bed and read a book of translations of Heraclitus and Diogenes. It gave her peace and calm. It was the first time all day that she was not hurting from last night's encounter. She had seen a film with Mark that they both had not liked and left before it was over. Then they had a drink in the hotel where they'd first spent time together. But this time, she found she was not interested in what he had to say. He was ponderous and she seemed to have no tolerance for chitchat. All that came clear to her was that she did not love him. He was an antidote to Kurt's unkindness. She suddenly saw she was being unfair to

Mark. She didn't want to go around hurting people like she was going around getting hurt. She must end it.

She read: Men dig up and search through much earth to find gold.

One wrong will not balance another: to be honorable and just is our only defense against men without honor or justice. Diogenes.

The greatest beauty of humankind is frankness.

Give up philosophy because I am an old man? It's at the end of a race that you break into a burst of speed.

God bless literature, she felt.

She had to read students' work and it saddened her because it was rarely poetic and so she must starve for a bit. But she could slip into these great works and it was good.

On their trip to the sea, she and Kurt had read together in their separate chairs each day. He had read a thriller and she read about a Jewish woman after the Holocaust. Stories of people surviving horror or not surviving.

Kurt then switched to reading newspapers. She went onto a book by Rilke about Cezanne.

"It's amazing what you read," he said.

"What do you mean?"

"You're so old fashioned," he said.

She assumed he meant the books were not au courant.

Kurt was surrounded by both serious and unserious au courant books in his apartment but she wondered if he read them all the way through or just bought them. A compulsion. He was a man of many compulsions, it turned out, movies, music, scotch, an ever array of expensive clothes, expensive toiletries, young chefs on the balcony, by the fire, in the kitchen, at his table. An exuberance of sensuality. He was autoerotic too.

"Lucia?"

"I'm in bed." Mira heard from within the apartment. That was odd because it was only 3 in the afternoon.

"Why?" Mira walked in. They both kept their doors open. They must be types who tempt fate, the good and the bad. They both wanted something unexpected to come through their doors. And, of course, Lucia had once been locked in with no way out. And now, Mira was locked up, by lack of courage.

She was standing in Lucia's living room. She heard from Lucia's bedroom, "I don't feel well."

"Shall I bring you dinner?"

"No."

"What's wrong?" Mira called out.

"A friend is being buried right now in this cold and I cannot go. I cannot even go to the memorial service tonight. Or go to my favorite Shabbos."

"Why not?"

"I am going to another friend later who is dying. I will sit with her. Everyone is dying, Mira."

Mira bent her head, her hand on the bedroom doorknob, but did not push it all the way open. She did not look in. That would be a different trespassing. One must not trespass on another's chrysalis. "I know. We all are," Mira answered. "How do you feel?"

"I don't know. Just weak, tired."

"Anything you need?"

"Live now, live intensely," Lucia called out.

Mira said nothing, hurting inside.

"Yes?" Lucia called out again, for a confirmation.

Mira smiled. She didn't want to let herself back out the door, saying "See you later," or "No," or "Maybe," or "I don't know," or "I don't want to."She really didn't.

"Yes, Lucia, I will."

She left on that note, that F major chord of "yes." May it change my DNA, she thought, as she tread quietly back downstairs.

CHAPTER 22

Mark would pick her up at the bus station, a bus being the most efficient way, he said, to his house. They had gone back and forth, she had liked the idea of working on a train, but it was very expensive and the station was not near his house in Maryland. She sat next to an Israeli woman on the bus who spoke continually on the phone to her husband, who was also waiting at the bus station.

Mira did not know what to expect when she would finally get there. Would she be bored? Would they have anything in common? Would they get on?

Last night she had slept at Kurt's but again he did not want to be touched. One does not get everything one wants, she told herself. It is part of being in relationship. She had noticed that her friends who began to accept that they did not get everything they wanted, started to get everything they wanted.

There had not been enough time in her life for music, lately. So she tuned into the music of the road.

Her mind began traveling. Messiaen wrote his greatest work in a concentration camp. Mahler while dying. Beethoven while deaf. Mozart while broke. Probably all of them while broke although Mahler was conducting. So Mahler worked while busy, as they all did. Busy and handicapped. Their relationships were what suffered.

Music. The last quartets for all of these composers were sonorous. Would the next work of Mira's be her last quartets? No. So many kept writing in their elder years passionately.

"You must work harder," Kurt said. "These are your golden years. Get up earlier." Although he had no idea when she did get up.

She was shy when Mark pulled the car up beside her. She had never seen him in a car. He was wearing a Russian hat, a dark coat. She didn't know what to say as she put her suitcase in the back of his car, a modest car, a car of a man who was not showy. They drove in the afternoon to his house that turned out to be very large and full of dark wood and chintzy curtains, but had many windows and it was comfortable, furnished in the old fashioned dark furniture that he explained "was Mom and Dad's," and what was unusual was that the house was museum-full of art. Even a Rembrandt. An El Greco. Remingtons. A Dali. De Pietros. The dining room made her think she was in the Uffizi. One Virgin after another.

"My father had lots of money," he said shyly.

She said nothing.

"They would get stolen in New York so I keep them here," he explained.

"Why do you think that?"

"Long story. When I was married and living in Boston, my ex got involved in stealing them from me through a lover."

"Really?"

"It was a whole disaster but anyway they are also a sort of cover for me. Everyone is taken with them so I don't have to talk about myself. I don't want to hide behind them everywhere. That said, I also never wanted everyone in New York knowing that I even have them."

She still said nothing.

"Also I don't want to break up the collection. I plan to donate them to a museum or John Hopkins when I die."

"Ah."

First, he walked and talked her through every painting. She found out, as they stood before a painting of Mark as a young man in a grey business suit, how it was that Dali did his portrait (for money, of course.) "Dali was interested in science and wanted to talk the physics of the universe," Mark said.

Then Mark made her a drink, offered her a choice of two excellent scotches and he gave her a little of each so she could choose, and they sat by his fireplace. They talked easily but seriously. They were trying to figure each other out. They talked for hours. He was married, twice; it turned out, which he had never brought up in New York. In the city, they had talked about music and her many ways of avoiding him. Here he was willing to reveal these convoluted stories betraying his fear of women being after his money. She listened carefully.

He said, "Let's go to dinner."

They went to a restaurant with a fireplace, which she was glad about since he did not put the heat up in his house, and they talked some more. She was not sure what to make of anything. He was gentlemanly in the restaurant, even in his house, but he had also been so in New York. Here he was making more of an effort since it was his turf and only his turf.

She didn't laugh, as she was wont to do with Kurt, Kurt and his creative ways of not having a real conversation.

They came home. "Do you want to sleep in my bed or in your own room?" Mark asked.

"My own room."

Kurt always with her. Or at least he was tonight.

"I knew that," he said. "I am an intellectual artifact."

"Don't say that," she answered.

"Okay, you can only take so much intimacy."

"More accurate," she replied.

He tried to kiss her. She liked that he tried. She liked that he held her close, she liked that he saw her as a woman and not a prop propping him up to be larger than he was.

"There is an electric blanket in your room," he said and he switched it on for her. She had never slept with an electric blanket and her room was pretty with its own bathroom. He left.

In the morning he brought in a tray he had prepared with strawberries and cheese and coffee. He placed it on her bed. It was lovely to be treated so well. He sat on the bed and chatted with her and she delighted in the coffee and bits of cheese.

Then he left the room so she could dress.

Once she came downstairs, they began the same itinerary as the day before. They talked all day and he watched her as she sat on the couch. He watched her as she sometimes took breaks to look at her computer and what she had to do. He simply sat across from her and took her in. He is a scientist, she told herself, he is looking at the proof.

What did he see? she wondered. He would tell her she is beautiful, but he must see, she thought, he must notice that I do not cleave to him. I don't smile in the right way; I don't walk over and touch him.

That night she had a dream where Kurt told her he no longer loved her. It was over. Yes, he said, he did sometimes sleep with his staff. There were many people working in his apartment. In the dream, his secretary ended up telling her he was having her investigated for past infidelities.

The next day before she took the bus back, Mark drove her to the station and got her a coffee for the road. She was moved watching him walk slowly in search of a coffee as she kept her place in the bus line and she watched him bring it over and hand it to her. The tenderness of it, the kindness, broke her heart.

CHAPTER 23

Her young student called to tell her that a grade B college offered him $10,000 in cash even before his receiving financial aid.

"But you have an interview with Harvard. Wait and see what Harvard says," she responded.

"Ten thousand dollars," he repeated.

"If you go to Harvard you'll earn 300,000 dollars a year."

He laughed.

"You're in demand," she said.

She had a thing against this grade B school. She wanted him to have the best. When did she turn into a bourgeois like this, she wondered? She was acting like those parents who wanted their child to do what they couldn't. She should have just been happy for him.

She was annoyed with herself. When will she ever act normally, she wondered.

All these years she thought she was good with people and it may be another delusion. Kurt liked to tell her she would be difficult on a full time basis, although she believed he would be even worse. That was when she alluded she wanted to live together. He always said no.

There was a burning alive today of a Jordanian pilot. She wrote Kurt, How can we get revenge?

He did not answer.

Maybe he was busy or maybe he liked to take his revenge out on her.

His revenge for all the women who have burned him.

She called her student back and told him she was proud of him. "I handled it badly," she said.

He said, "I totally get it."

Where did a wonderful boy like this come from?

If only she could meet a grown up version of him. Smart, wise, emotional, loving. He was a prince. How many princes would she ever know?

"Mom said the same thing," he said.

"I am sure."

A year ago a woman saying she was a producer had wanted to produce a work of Mira's. They met often and planned what they needed to do and it took maybe 11 months for Mira to break the blindness of her desire and see the woman was not delivering on any of her promises. Mira could not figure out what all those talks had been about. Maybe if you talk production, it is enough. Finally, Mira stopped contact, feeling a fool. Why did she attract, she wondered, people who did not treat her respectfully? Why did people not go the distance for her?

A year later, the producer got in touch again. Mira had not found anyone else. Kurt and Mira's best friend said, "Forget her, the producer is a charlatan."

But Mira, after many attempted contacts from the producer, decided to meet her again. She didn't have any expectations, was just curious about what the producer would say.

Her name was Margarida and she agreed to meet in a local, quiet bar next to Mira's apartment where they had often met in the old days. Mira figured, at least it is close by.

When Mira walked in, she slid into a seat next to Margarida. The producer was younger than Mira, chunky with a pretty face, and sharp quick eyes that always seemed a bit nervous.

Margarida said, "I want to do it now."

"You would have to put together a contract this time and really go into action," Mira said. "Hire people. Commit to it. We wasted enough time already. I can't go through the disappointment again."

"I know."

For some reason, Mira, as she studied Margarida's bulldog face, decided to believe her. She recollected people in the theater telling her, "All producers are crazy." "The path is always fraught with frustrations." Mira didn't ask for an explanation for why now or why not then, perhaps Margarida's other projects had drained her too much. Who knew? This producer understood her work. Maybe Mira knew all along that eventually Margarida would come through. Maybe these horses that are long shots do come through. Maybe Mira knew more than she thought.

"I am sending you a contract tomorrow for the option," Margarida said, and they shook hands and celebrated. They were going to make something, as Mira felt life was all about, and Mira, once again, felt that it would happen.

Kurt had made so much fun of Margarida in the dance before where Margarida had never come through that she could not tell him that the producer she was working with was her. He would say Mira was an idiot to believe her this time but, a week later, Margarida did end up signing a contract, paying the option and hiring a General Manager and Director to put the play on. Now they had to raise the money.

Kurt, who had excelled at Yale, U Penn and in business, did not understand that not everything is past performance, that there are race horses who come in unexpectedly. He did not understand that people can change for the better. He did not understand that you don't always get exactly what you want when you want it.

This progress, if it was to be progress, happened, she realized, because she didn't take revenge.

CHAPTER 24

Back when she had been in Barcelona, after the French Jew returned to Jerusalem and she had stayed on alone, she walked the beach in the sun. That was where she reflected on the word, magnetism. She had been by herself on the beach, there weren't many people on it, and she had felt entirely full, alive.

The sea felt magnetic.

To the kissing on the rocks when she was a girl in blue by the sea. The magnetism in Barcelona. Even with Kurt, so many times sitting next to him on a beach. As always, he closed his eyes, shut her out, but she felt him next to her and she heard the music of that soft gentle return. He probably had gone to the beach with many women, as she had done with many men, the eternal triangle. A man, woman and the sound of the sea.

But she knew if she got near the sea again, she would think more clearly.

Her essence would begin to begin again. She would come close to this music, call it into her, and then she would meet a man whose body could be her own.

She would become magnetic again.

She would hear herself.

When the music and the sea were inside her, she would lean into a man and kiss him. Good god, Lucia was right about a kiss pulling you forward, she thought years later as she remembered that beach. All the songs ever written would play at once and, she would love and give herself.

That was magnetism. The merging. People she loved. Kindnesses. Touch. The melody of the world around us.

Inside.

CHAPTER 25

That same day, Mira was walking up the yellow stairs to her apartment when a neighbor stopped her.

"Did you know Lucia is in hospital?"

Mira held her breath and said, "Where?"

Mira quickly took a $30 cab to Columbia Presbyterian, all the way uptown.

"What are you doing here?" Lucia asked, when Mira walked in.

Lucia was bruised and her hands and legs were swollen. She was attached to all kinds of IVs. Mira was shocked at the contrast between Lucia's misshapen body and Lucia's generous, girlish smile.

"More importantly, what are you doing here? "Mira asked,

sitting down in the one chair next to the bed.

Lucia said, "I've been thinking how everyone says they had a traumatic childhood."

"That's why you're in hospital?" Mira smiled, and then looked around at a tray where Lucia had eaten nothing.

"I'm ill, of course."

"What's wrong?"

"I don't know yet."

Mira wondered if Lucia was lying.

"I'm 89," Lucia said. "That's what's wrong."

Mira had figured that out from Lucia's book. "They'll get you better," Mira said.

"Will they now?"

"Yes."

A nurse came in to adjust an IV. Lucia was uncharacteristically silent. The nurse left.

"If people did not get enough religion, it was traumatic. If they got too much, it was traumatic," Lucia said.

It was amazing to Mira that she would be thinking of these kinds of things. But maybe to rail against life is to be alive. To rail is to feign power against so much that we are powerless against and right now, for Lucia, it was her body.

"I know," Mira answered. "I never quite saw my own childhood as traumatic. I saw it all as material."

Lucia said, "You're original, that's why."

"This is not a time to think about me," Mira responded.

"Why not?"

"Lucia, what do you need?"

She looked at Mira intently with her dark eyes. Lucia had a strange bruise on her face.

"Did you fall?"

"Yes."

"When?"

"Why do we have to have these talks?"Lucia asked brusquely.

"What do you want to talk about?"

"Are you living the life you want?"

"Mostly. It's not nirvana but pretty close," Mira answered.

Lucia closed her eyes. "Exactly," she said.

"Lucia?"

"Lucia?"

Mira jumped at the remote by Lucia's bed and pushed, pushed all the buttons. Then she ran out into the hallway just as a nurse was running toward her. She followed the nurse into the room. Her pulse. Her temples. "I am sorry," the nurse said, with a gentle solemnity that she must put on for all these occasions.

Mira instantly began to cry.

De do dum dum de do dum dum. She is using the beat of some a Capella group to calm herself down. At least she thinks that's what it is.

She realized as she cried how deeply Lucia was inside her. Suddenly they were handing Mira papers to sign.

"I'll look in her things, for information," Mira explained, not touching the papers. "I am not her kin but I live in the same apartment building."

"Who is her kin?"

Mira swallowed.

"Whom do I call when I get you the information?" Mira asked, deflecting.

Mira was handed a bevy of phone numbers.

She left the hospital, heartbroken and did something she had never done before. She called Kurt.

"I am sorry," he said. "I know you loved her. You were good to her."

She said a few incoherent things and somehow they got disconnected. She did not call him back. She was too discombobulated and she wanted to be alone with thoughts of Lucia.

Lucia, she realized, living in her building, upstairs, with their conversations that flowed in and out, like the ocean, had been magnetism too.

CHAPTER 26

When she got back to her apartment, she sat at her desk, stunned, and listened to Les McCann, and she heard those exquisite keyboard riffs and remembered that the last time she saw Les McCann, he couldn't play. He'd had a stroke and lost all his abilities, but the jazz club booked him because he must have needed the money. He had given so much pleasure in his career that people came just out of respect for all the happiness he had rhythmed out in his life. He had been a great, a wizard at the keyboard of energy and joy.

She hadn't gone upstairs to Lucia's yet. Instead, she sat in her own apartment and thought more about Les McCann. How she had felt inexorably sad, as she had sat that night in the audience. She had always loved him, even met him in a jazz club once. He had touched her breasts, she had only been eighteen, returning from the ladies room and he was coming out of that room musicians go to between sets, and he reached down and put his hand through the opening in her dress and squeezed her breast. Then he went on stage with his band. They didn't exchange any words and she didn't even think about it then; she was solely focused on the exuberance of his playing. To her mind, he was allowed any liberty for such talent.

When Lucia's life had been all said and done, at the end, she gave herself to her own talent, a talent for resilience, kindness and seeing.

Mira took a bath and read Adorno who wrote that when artists decide to live off their own work, they begin to turn out dross. But that's not true she told herself. Look at Dali. Picasso. Roth, no matter how you wanted to get angry at him, the cat could write and he wasn't pandering, she thought, to the public.

She was avoiding going upstairs.

She hated the literalness of death. One was left with someone's "things." It was vaguely an insult to Lucia. Things without the person were an effrontery.

It must be the spirit. Life must be the spirit.

Although Mark, scientist that he was, was confounded when she said she observed the Jewish holidays. He thought Mira must go to synagogue to be part of the community, rather than for spiritual reasons, and maybe he was right. She remembered the last Yom Kippur and the Rabbi had opened the ceremony saying he did not believe in a god who lets this one live, the other one die.

Mira was not sure there was any other religion with a high holiday that began with how they did not believe in the God whom everyone was taught to believe in.

That was why she loved Judaism.

In that conversation with Mark, where he had been sitting in his house as he watched her, she had broken from whatever else they were talking about and said, "You are saying that in your scientific study there is proof of no god, right?"

"I am."

Old boyfriends would have come over to help her now with Lucia's apartment. Mark would most likely if she asked him because she was sure he was a mensch. Kurt wouldn't think of it.

Whom would she talk to now when everything is bedrock?

Tempus fugit.

She went upstairs. The place was a mess. The nurse had told

Mira that Lucia herself called an ambulance to get her.

"Why I wonder," Mira said.

The nurse had gone to the file to look and Mira followed her. "She complained of not feeling right." Lucia, Mira thought, and her understatement.

She must no longer have believed in a kiss.

She went through Lucia's desk looking for a will, for an address book to let people know. She had never had a death talk with Lucia. Mira's friend Sally said to Mira, "You have to give me a power of attorney, a will, all of that."

"I am not ready," Mira replied.

"You don't know when you're going to die," Sally said.

"I am not ready for all that yet," Mira repeated.

Mira's plan was to wait till she was 70 before she admitted to her own death. Give me these years of reprieve. Other people die right now, not her, she told herself, like she was a god. Anyway Sally had euthanized her cat too quickly. In Mira's opinion, the cat simply was ill with something that could pass. Sally was the type who expedited.

Mira found an address book filled in Lucia's small, neat European handwriting. The landlord must also have information, Mira realized. There were names in the book. She would call them and begin a type of detective work. As she walked back downstairs, she feared the most that no one would care when they got the call.

She broke up calling the names on the address pages between her own obligations. Lucia's husband's family, there were people. Mira was given more names and numbers. They would make calls for her. "Yes, how terrible, but is there any money?" running through their voices. Mira had no idea.

"There must be a will somewhere," Mira said.

She called the hospital and said she'd be in touch in a day. Lucia's body was waiting in ice storage. "We are trying to arrange a funeral. I will know in 24 hours."

She put the phone down.

Ravel piano music in the background pulling her, like a vortex, pulling her towards life. Somehow the CD jumped to Seal, "colors fade to gray, good times today." She had been with the prisoner in a shop when she heard Seal's music the first time. She went to the cashier and asked what it was.

The next week, broke as he was in a halfway house, she received the CD in the mail. He had sent it to her. Sent her the music.

The music.

If only she could tell Lucia that she had been wrong. Sometimes it is nirvana.

CHAPTER 27

Strangely no one did show up at Lucia's apartment right away but Mira was sure someone would. If not, she would handle it herself. In the following days, as she walked to dinners, plays, meetings and the snow fell down lightly in the sun, she noted that life goes on. Friends asked her for dinner and she found herself sitting there alone in groups, but then she always had been sitting alone. Kurt never wanted to go. He needed time to renew himself, he said. He needed to be alone to read, to sleep. Did she have any idea the pressure he was under?

Her buzzer rang.

A tall man began climbing her stairs. A navy coat. A suit,

tie. No one dressed like this was even usually seen in this bohemian neighborhood. This must have to do with Lucia. It seemed business like.

"Yes?"

"This is Lucia's building, right?" he asked in a British accent.

"Yes. Um . . ." Mira began. How would she break the sad news in a tasteful manner?

"I know," he said. "She is dead. I am, in a long convoluted way, related."

Why hadn't Lucia told her she had such a marvelous looking relative?

"Do you have a key?" Mira asked, trying to figure out if he was indeed related.

"Yes. I rang because I wanted to alert someone what I was doing and not just some man breaking in."

"Thoughtful of you and very non New York," she smiled. "Sensitive." Enough of this, Mira, since he is stunningly attractive. To her. The slender elegance. The intelligent blue eyes. The even voice that had a tinge, she was sure, of humor behind it. "Okay, let me know if I can help," she said. Then she stopped. "Do you want some tea? Coffee?"

He looked at her. "No thanks."

That was good. She didn't have any.

He was about to go upstairs and then he stopped and turned around. "I'm supposed to go through her things and decide what to do," he said rather seriously, and as if he was frightened. "Also make the arrangements."

"Oh."

He smiled a bit. "I hate this kind of thing. You end up throwing out someone's life. Most of it has no meaning for anyone else. So you end up putting it in the rubbish. It's horrible except it will happen to me too so I guess it all evens out in the end."

Imagine, she thought, an Englishman with feelings.

"Yes," she said. "Did you know Lucia well? She was quite wonderful."

"Yes she knew my mother. My mother and she were very good friends. Both from Austria. Both . . . you know . . ."

"I take it your mother survived."

"In her way," he said.

She smiled and looked intently at his face. It was almost the first time she looked at him full face, had the courage to. It made her realize how timid she is in love. She saw intelligence. Thin lips. Those very communicative blue eyes. Almost the face of an actor.

"Well, pop by if you want to talk after," she said. Was she making a pass at him? He probably has a young girlfriend like the rest of the world.

"Thank you," he said as he climbed the stairs.

She went to her desk to distract herself from wondering what was going on up there. He should have asked her out for dinner, she thought, amusing herself with her usual fantasies.

She went to her email. There was a note from Mark, asking her why she had never considered marrying him. That was a rhetorical question resulting from a previous email where she had rhetorically wondered why she herself had never remarried, like her ex had done.

"But then," she had written in her email, "you, Mark, haven't married either. Why haven't you?"

He had replied," You'll get your answer if you ask yourself why you have never considered marrying me."

An answer from a scientist. Look to the proof.

Fifteen minutes later it seemed, Bill, Lucia's relative, came to her door.

"Come in, come in," she said, thinking to herself, And don't ever leave. Oh Lucia help me now. I want to open up, I do.

"You don't need to get me anything," he said, sitting on her couch. He seemed to make the room look more elegant. He would be good, she thought, as a piece of art in her apartment.

"So you knew Lucia well?" he asked.

"Yes. I loved her. She was, in her way, spiritual, even after . . . you know . . . she had a loving nature. Someone recently told me that survivors are all bitter, and I ended up disagreeing. So much so that I never wanted to see that person again."

"Really?" He looked at her quickly, to try and figure out, she assumed, if she is crazy.

Maybe she is, she thought, and continued, "Yes, I guess bitterness as the only response infuriated me. I don't believe it is the only response to evil and Lucia embodied that it isn't."

Now his regard became a little bit more relaxed since he sat back on her couch and started to breathe. He clearly did not like this assignment from his mother. And Mira, Mira had now got herself on a roll.

"I have two theories on this whole issue of response to evil," she continued, unasked, standing across the room from him. "One is that some people's sense of ethics are larger than the evil they witness and so they are able to recover. In other words, their ethics make them have a type of distance from those who don't have any ethics or that some people have so much creativity in them that they are buoyant, no matter what fate deals them, and they have to make something of it."

He said nothing, listening.

"Although," Mira said, "it is hard for me to forget the whole thing, like everyone else can't. How could anyone throw a baby into a fire? But I don't know if I am bitter. I am appalled and must do good, I think."

She was talking to herself and then came back to the present, "I'm sorry. I don't know why I am getting so incensed."

He was quiet, thinking. He had the British way of not being inattentive, but not looking at a person intrusively.

She then asked, "Did you know her well?" She didn't remember Lucia ever mentioning him.

"No, that's because I haven't lived in this country till about 4 months ago and I haven't made the effort to see her. She really was my mother's friend."

"Yes."

"But my mother so respected her and loved her that I feel sort of tied to her. And I did see her as a child. She was quite beautiful, you know."

"Till the end."

"I, in fact, as a boy was always ashamed of finding her attractive."

"Was it her looks or who she was?" Mira asked.

"Her looks, I am sure. I didn't notice who women were at that age!" he laughed. "I am afraid young boys are run by hormones, not intellectual communication."

"Eternally," she said.

He smiled.

"So I don't quite understand," Mira said," how is it you have a key etcetera and have the job of going through her things?"

"She left everything to my mother who is too old to go through everything and also I suppose I will end up with it all anyway. "

"What about her husband's family?"

"I don't know. Maybe she felt closer to my mother, with them going further back to her childhood. Her husband's family may not have cared. I don't know. I am sorry."

Mira, say something human. Something vulnerable. Don't hide just because you find him attractive.

"Are you married?" she asked.

"No. Not now," he smiled.

Christ, she's smiling like the Japanese girl.

"So you now live in New York?" she asked. "Do you like it?"

"Yes." He shifted now to look more directly at her, as if this topic was safer. "It's like there's some ozone on the pavement that makes everyone excitable, more intense than in other cities. Even London. There you have quiet. Here everything is on speed."

"Yes. It becomes addictive," she answered and then said, "Lucia loved New York. Her walks in the park. The opera. She was always going to music. Flowers in her apartment. The museums, she always knew what shows were on. Reading the op ed pages . . ."

Mira loved New York, too. It was starting. He was bringing it on. Just his presence. She began to cry.

"What is it?"

"Lucia. She was so . . ." she said, crying. "So kind. And brave. And funny. She loved to laugh. She would get a kick out of making fun of me," she said. "And that generation. They are going."

He got up and put his hand on her shoulder. And that made her cry more.

"My mother said she cried too when she found out," he offered, standing over her.

"Yes. You have no idea how wonderful she was. It isn't fair."

"She was 89," he said.

Who am I crying for Mira began to wonder.

She got hold of herself. "Yes," she said primly, "you're right, she was not young." So what, Mira thought.

He looked down at her and began fondling his watch.

And now she has lost whatever flicker of interest he might have had for her, she decided.

Where was Kurt? Why does everyone say he doesn't love her?

Who loves anyone? What is love?

"I don't know anything," she ended up saying to Bill. "I just don't know anything anymore." This is where vulnerability got her. Totally lost.

He was quiet for a minute.

"Nobody does." He hesitated and then said, "Would you mind," he asked, "writing a eulogy for her?"

Mira nodded her head, "I would love to, it would be an honor."

Now he was back to his management mode. She was back to pretending she was normal. He smiled at her and said, "I'll let you know where the memorial will be."

"You're taking care of it?" she asked. Was that smile of his politeness or could it possibly be understanding?

"I am. I should be off," he said. "Here is my card with my personal number on the back." She was curious as to what he did for a living. Now she would find out. "I will of course be in touch about everything, the funeral, the memorial, all of that. I have your details from upstairs."

That was clever, she thought.

"Thank you for helping her, " he said.

Mira put out her hand to shake his. "It would be awful not to."

"Well a lot of people didn't when they should have," he said.

"True," she said, so grateful he made that statement. This man, she thought, has sensitivity. Now it was she who smiled, as she nodded to him as he began his trek down the stairs.

CHAPTER 28

She was getting dressed to meet Kurt and his son and another one of her students whom she was fixing his son up with. She was nervous Kurt would get too excited by this 24 year old, dark haired, slender and Modigliani-faced student, as he was wont to do with young women.

She had seen photos of Kurt, when he was younger, with flashy looking blondes and brunettes. He must like that type. He himself was flashy in his $1000 shirts, ascots, Prada shoes.

She wore a short skirt and black sweater. She was just a dash of flash, she noted. A little of this, a little of that. No wonder she didn't know where she belonged.

His son had announced once on another visit to his father when Mira was sitting there, that his father had good taste in women. Was he giving Mira a compliment or referring to his father's past? His son had said that he didn't want to be with a beautiful woman, but a pretty one. Kurt answered, "Don't say that in front of her," as if the son was talking about Mira.

She almost couldn't forgive him.

The constant humiliation. Or was it hers towards herself?

But at dinner Kurt sat with his arm around her, warm, and cheerfully talking away. He was happy in a restaurant with her and his son, happy talking to a lovely pretty woman that Mira had brought.

They had fun the four of them and then Kurt wanted to go home, his back and leg hurt. They dropped the two younger people off at a jazz club. In his apartment, they watched a bit of a movie as they usually did and he made himself busy placing a heating pad underneath himself. Naturally he moved her hand down to what might be his essence. She began by kissing his penis and then moved to be on top of him.

"More oral," he said.

"No," she answered.

And he laughed derisively at being caught out at always him,

him, and she got on top of him and remembered when she would get into cars with men, so young she was, and they would pull out their penises, out of uncontainable desire and she imagined right now she was in a car with Kurt wanting her as the young girl she had been.

Afterwards, he rearranged the heating pad.

"Do you want a back rub for your back?" she asked in the dark.

Immediately he turned over. "Yes."

She sat on his buttocks and tried to create distance between his vertebrae.

"You are divine," she heard in the blackness of the night. She must be, she thought, with how little she asks for herself.

In the morning, he got up earlier than usual to arrange breakfast for his son who was visiting for the weekend. Kurt was cheerful, busy, in a humorous mood. He even, he said, felt better.

The three of them chatted, Kurt holding a newspaper away from his face as he did so. She recommended a museum for his son to go see before he returned to Washington.

"I'll go make some more coffee," Kurt said, suddenly a barista.

"It's good to be home," the son said to her.

"Yes, it must be good for you to be here."

"No, I mean Washington," he answered. "I like my life there."

His father returned into the room, carrying little demitasses. "How come you did not stay at Madelin's?" he asked, "the girl last night?"

"She's nice, Dad, but I'm not rushing into something. We'll stay in touch."

Then Kurt said to his son, "I will take you to something tonight, if you stay over an extra night."

Mira admired and loved Kurt's caring for his son, but she noted he had never made that offer to her.

Mira noticed Kurt looking at her appraisingly in the morning in her short skirt and black loose sweater. He said nothing. Was it her fault that he was silent since she often sloughed off compliments? No, most man will give them if they feel them. They are driven to. It is their way of seducing, claiming. Even Kurt, she was sure. She had seen him do it before. Mostly to other women.

But why should she need constant compliments? Had he made her that insecure? Yes. It was ridiculous. What was it she was really needing?

She had asked him once when they were having dinner why he did not want her around too much.

He replied, "You're too distracting. You need too much attention."

She visited Mark the same evening she had left Kurt and his son. They had made a plan earlier in the week. They were still friendly, if not lovers. As she sat down in Mark's apartment, before dinner, he immediately launched into a conversation that shocked her.

"I need to get married," he said.

"What do you mean?"

"Because I have so much money."

"What?"

"It's about taxes," and he went into a convoluted discussion about giving his relatives 5 million tax-free but the rest of the estate gets taxed by the paintings. She was surprised he had such a large estate.

"But why are you thinking about that? You're not that old."

"I just am," he said. "And I don't want to be alone. I want a wife who is here. And who spends time with me in that house in the country. I want to sleep with someone and I want someone to take care of me, as I do of her."

It was sweet of him, it really was, she thought. He wanted to care for her. But what did he want in return? Someone who authentically was in love with him.

She sat there quietly stunned in the dark on his couch, their dinner reservations waiting and realized he was trying to cut a deal with her. But a woman who has never been interested in money is not the type to get seduced by money. She may dream of money but not enough to do something bizarre for it.

If that had been her intention, she would have done it by now.

She suddenly saw he was a man who may think about music and science, but he believed too much in the power of money. Suddenly her psyche began, at some meteoric pace, to run away from him.

So that's what she had been avoiding. She had sensed the lack of life in such a request.

They had a pleasant dinner but she was completely kerfuffled. She said, "We should not be discussing marriage at this stage of the game."

"I suppose," he answered, gangly and somewhat sheepishly. He now knew she knew he had been cutting a deal, she saw, in his slight awkwardness.

"Mark," she said, "I appreciate what you said and it is an honor, it really is, but I am just not suited to marriage. It's not your fault. I just never have been."

Was that true or an excuse?

She sipped her wine and now she felt hate for Kurt for never thinking of marriage and union with her, or her future, and then her mind switched to love for Kurt who had known that her passion was freedom and that was the thing he had given her, the only thing he gave her, or perhaps freedom was what they shared.

To make conversation, she told Mark that she had a friend whose boyfriend said he would never marry or live with her and maybe the reason was his money, she provoked.

"Maybe he doesn't want anyone getting at it," she posited. She was referring to Kurt. She really didn't know if that was true, she was just talking for the sake of it.

"Sounds like a horrible guy," Mark said.

She smiled to herself, affirmed in her suspicions.

"Maybe he is worried that she would squander his money," Mark added. This made her laugh inside. Mark must be talking about himself if he had thought of that. And yes, she could see Kurt doing that.

Mark wanted her to make love with him but after this discussion she could not. Anyway after that first time, she had stayed away from him. Her body was trained toward Kurt, Kurt who does not touch her.

She had recently told Kurt she wanted to live with someone (she meant him) and he said, "What are you going to do?"

That told her what he was going to do. Absolutely nothing. Next.

That night she left Mark, sad, which she explained to him as her not being able to get Lucia out of her mind. And she would have loved to talk this over with Lucia, who might have told her she was an idiot, which she knows she is, holding onto a with-holding man as she does.

She missed Lucia. But it was not the real reason she left Mark. If only Mark and she could have talked about things that interested her, but instead, he had moved on from money to past victories at work, people she would never meet. He did not know what films were out, what contemporary books, he was in his mind with Mahler and old journals. He was brilliant but maybe all along he had not been able to hold her interest.

He was tall and thin and beautiful in his disheveled intellectual way but she could not make love to a world that felt hemmed in by his and the world's past. Even though, in loving Kurt, she was making love to what was missing in her own past. By loving Kurt, she returned to the existential place of hurt and loss. Over and over.

Admittedly, Mark wanted to take her somewhere new, and that was good, but he had made an offer as if love was a transaction and, without even understanding it, she had scoured away.

CHAPTER 29

She played the last movement of Mahler's 3rd on her CD player. She hadn't even turned the music off when a woman who made her living as a live-in caretaker for elderly women came in for help with her story.

This woman sat in Mira's living room and told her she wanted to write a famous book about her mother in Kenya and her own life in the slums and out of them.

Mahler driving rhythmically in the background.

"Yes, yes," Mira said to the woman, "there is a story there but writing is difficult."

"How can it be made into a film?" the woman asked, her eyes

glowing with hope.

"It's highly unlikely," Mira explained. "Many good stories do not make it into films and there is no guarantee. You have to write this story if it is burning in your heart for yourself."

"Yes, yes," she said.

"Why," the woman asked, "do I have this drive, this feeling that something is inside me? I know you are not a psychologist," the woman said, "but why?"

This while Mira's friend had just died. Yes, why?

"Because you do have a story," Mira said. "It is a great story of someone achieving, making a life against all odds."

The woman went on to tell her how amazing her mother in Kenya was. It was not her real mother but this woman was so good to her, and strong. She knew things psychically.

Mira nodded.

When the session was over, Mira refused money. "It's a gift to you and your mother."

This woman had already told her that the person she was caretaking was 101 years old and rich and rude to her. She was the first black woman that this old woman had ever met. Mira knew this woman's life was hard.

The woman got very happy at saving money. She felt loved, blessed. And that was a gift for Mira.

The woman started rustling about and wanted to give Mira a hug.

It's really for Lucia, Mira thought, as she let herself be clasped in those big and tender arms. An offering.

Once she was alone, Mira turned the music up loud and waited for the drums to come in at the end of the Mahler symphony. The strings had gone on as sublime and spiritual as they could and the horns were calling out proudly, powerfully to the heart, and the strings vibrated a response, and the horns started to come in again, strong, resonant, and the drums began, the heartbeat loud, thump thump thump thump, thump thump, thump as the purity of the strings and the call of the horns set the tone, the base, the platform for the beat of the heart.

CHAPTER 30

Two days later, she and Kurt had dinner with his chef. This young girl seemed a bit plain, with her hair in a severe ponytail, and she was less intelligent, and a touch passive, so this one interested him not as much as others. Thus he was less flirtatious with her.

Mira wore one of her student's dresses and he said he didn't like the color but he liked the cut. "Because," he said, "Mira, you have a good figure."

He was upset Mira was going away for 2 weeks on business to a client who lived by the sea in South America. She was off to help this woman write her memoir.

"What if you meet a caballero? They are lounge lizards and

will be in the hotel," he said.

She didn't want to reply that they most likely wouldn't be interested in a woman of her age.

He said, "You're still valuable, even for an old broad."

She teasingly flashed reproving eyes at him.

He said, "You used to always call yourself that."

She did refer to herself years ago, when they first knew each other, as an old broad, when she had the confidence to think it was funny because she was not yet an old broad.

Later that night, when they were alone by the fireplace, she said, "I don't understand why you refuse to live with me when you have lived with other women."

He immediately looked nervous and said, "I don't want to talk about that. I am happy with the way things are. It is working."

They kept putting wood on the fire.

Dinner was excellent and she felt joy looking at him, at hearing his non sequitur thoughts about his work, about the music he played, about the chef's cooking, about what was going on in the news. He loved the news as a way to not discuss personal matters.

It was all friendly and comfortable but the next morning as she was leaving, she saw on her phone that she was overdrawn in her account. She was away from her real life in Kurt's home, a reprieve from her difficulties. No wonder she wanted to live there.

"I need to know phone numbers for where you are going," he said, "in case something happens to you."

She was touched by that.

He was acting like a husband, a bit.

In bed, he moved her hand down to him as always and she said, "Let's do something different."

"Why?" he answered, and she once again realized predictability was everything to him.

After he fell asleep, she listened to the sound of his sleeping. Unlike her, he could relax and sleep when she had her arm around him. It was she who could not sleep when someone had their arm around her.

Note this, Mira, note this. Who is the one who is difficult?

Celestial voices in Mahler's *Resurrection*. To life. "L'Chaim," Kurt always said before a cocktail. Mahler used voices in the symphony as percussion. The horns now affirm the voices, as yes, we are going up, up. We are proclaiming our rise. The drums underscore it, but the horns slow down and then blare, affirm, affirm, affirm, as the drums roll and roll yes.

And now the 4th. The most Austrian of his work to her, a touch of a waltz, a touch of the world being orderly, not Mahler's usual counterpoints. Just a waltz to begin. Almost Mozartian.

And then she listened at her desk to the 9th which Mahler's daughter, a sculptor in Paris, loved the most, as did Mira. Its lyrical beginning. Her father, Mira was sure, was gentle, loving, to write such delicate and powerful music. When asked to sum up her famous femme fatale mother in one word, Mahler's daughter answered, "Envy."

The ninth, the last full symphony he wrote.

Lucia had once told her that she had been depressed lately, and she could not write anymore. Mahler feared death for only that reason, that he could no longer work. Beryl Bainbridge writing in her hospital room before she died. Jean Rhys could no longer write when she was old, so she sustained what was left of herself by talking about the mechanics of writing. Mira remembered that Lucia had a radio by her bed in the hospital. She also remembered Lucia saying of her friend who died that year, "She had music on as she drifted off."

The horns in the ninth ask questions. The horns ask, What is this? And the tubas answer, It is lilting, but never forget that it is somber.

Mira was waiting in the airport for her flight to go to the sea in Uruguay. She would give Lucia's eulogy when she returned. There was no music in the airport. Men no longer looked at her or tried to meet her. It saddened her although she had always resented the constant interruption in the days when it did happen. "Where are you going?" "What do you do?" "Where are you staying?" Usually the men were incredibly boring.

She had been angry with Kurt that morning. He took a long shower and then came upstairs to prepare breakfast for himself. He made his tea and only after, her coffee. She was not allowed to use the coffee machine. While she had been waiting for him, she had seen a note on his piano. Make dinner reservations. She had written next to it, "With whom?"

"Did you see something incriminating, honey?" he laughed at her. That was the thing. He could read her mind. Maybe it was the seriousness on her face.

"Yes."

"What?"

"You'll see. I left a note," she said.

He made breakfast, she tried to help by unloading the dishwasher, "You're a good worker, honey," he said and they discussed inanities and they both wanted her to go. But she also wanted him to say something romantic before she left.

Last night she had told him about a friend of hers (it was herself) where a man wanted to marry her for financial reasons. Her friend is poor, she said, but she doesn't want to do it.

"She should do it," he said.

"She doesn't love him."

"So what? And anyway he loves her. Her future will be taken care of. She may regret it when she is older."

"She doesn't want to sleep with him."

"Why not?" he asked.

"She doesn't love him."

"You and I have both slept with people we weren't in love with."

"Well let's go look at this incriminating evidence," he had said cheerfully after breakfast.

She showed him "Make dinner reservations." He saw her note, "With whom?"

"That's a note to make dinner reservations when I am in Miami with my son. As I did when we went to Florida. You know I do that."

"Oh."

She wasn't sure she believed him.

She had her coat on. She had to get ready for her trip. They should be living together.

He walked her to the door. "This jealousy of yours is pathological," he said.

"Yes."

"Have you seen the movie *Gaslight?*" he asked.

"That doesn't help your case," she said.

"I know," he answered. He was standing at his door. "Well don't drink the water. Be careful what you eat. Be careful what you put into your mouth," he said smiling.

"Kurt," she said.

He loved his joke.

"Bye," she said.

Later, as she was packing, she emailed him that she was upset at leaving him for so long. It had unglued her a bit. He didn't respond. Then she sent him her addresses in South America.

She hurt all day that he didn't contact her till finally she got an email at the airport, "What airline are you flying?"

Checkmate.

CHAPTER 31

She landed in Buenos Aries in the early morning of a night sky, got a cab in what seemed a small, busy chaotic airport and the cab drove her through silent damp, shining, grand streets, broken up by huge parks and sculptures. She felt suddenly free.

Just after breakfast, she visited a beautiful graveyard, with sculptures everywhere and hundred-year-old trees, and then a gold and aristocratic opera house. After, she and the woman she had come to visit, Sara, grey haired with flashing dark eyes, walked a bit in this elegant open city. Sara's book was about rescuing the girl inside herself who had been left alone, parentless, growing up on a kibbutz, raised or not raised by the other children, rather than a mother. Sara needed someone to assist her as she told her story. She needed a mother now.

The following day, Mira and Sara took a boat to Montevideo.

Mira felt exuberantly happy on the ferry. She could not go far enough away from her life. Everything was new, changed, as Whitehead advocated for happiness.

When the ferry docked in Montevideo, Mira stepped out into this quiet, proud city on the sea, unspoiled and separate. This city that did not scream commercialism and obsession with money, just apartments with big windows overlooking trees, and no Starbucks with its messy, long lines of people on cell phones or wearing backpacks that hit you in the face. She walked past out-of-fashion shoe shops, office buildings that looked like apartments. She felt for the first time in so long, full and whole. Sea-swept Montevideo in Uruguay, on a hill, old, captured the artist in her. The poetry was in its being what it was, not gentrified into every other city. She walked around the crumbling streets and the wide squares with ancient beautiful trees, the huge painterly working port that had not been turned into a shopping mall like so many had in other cities, and she felt that excitement in her chest that is called falling in love. There was not the culture or glamor of New York but there was the realness of the streets. Because of that, art lived here. There was time for it. She was sure intellectuals and writers and artists were hiding in these apartments. Remote South America suddenly seemed the place for her to be found. She had waited to know where and of course it would be somewhere like her own self, undiscovered, crumbling but insisting in vain on its own failing independence and purity.

Europe was eternal with its problems that were repetitions, she decided. This continent, because it was far away, and nobody knew how to treat it, was new. And why had two books she had been hired to work on been about South America? A coincidence? Maybe not, she now wondered.

She walked the cobbled streets taking in the stately unadorned buildings, an opera house of their own. Kurt had sent no word. He had been to South America before. With other women. He allegedly had fallen in love in Buenos Aries.

She watched the sea from the old broken car that Darlene, Sara's friend, was driving to take them to a seaside town. Most of the cars in Uruguay seemed from another time. Darlene, Sara's friend, with long grey blonde hair and a beautiful smile, had the sensuality and freedom of someone who had built her own life. The sea constantly on their right. The sea from the hillside, the sea out the window.

Mira remembered the time before when she had saved herself this very same way, by moving to the sea. It was when she realized that her mother who had abandoned her as a child would never love her. The pain was so much that she went off and stopped her life and rented an apartment on a cove. She took walks to beaches, rode her bike around and men left flower bouquets tied to the handlebars. She intuitively knew that beauty, as Dostoyevsky said, would heal her. It would hold her, as life had not yet. That was when she met her husband.

The inchworm inches.

How was it she was even in this beauty now, here? She had taken a weekly seminar in New York on great philosophical and poetic and religious and psychoanalytical work. The attendants at the seminar read assigned work and discussed them. She loved the readings.

There, not surprisingly, she met a woman interested in self-discovery who lived part-time in Uruguay. She had married a Uruguayan and he wanted to retire there. It was the perfect quiet place to write a book about rescuing the abandoned girl inside her and Sara hired Mira to help.

And here, it was Mira who was being rescued by the feminine. Venus as she Ages. Born of the sea.

CHAPTER 32

Sitting in her hotel room, with the sea golden out the window, and an island of seals in the corner of her eye, she made a plan.

She would stop worrying. She would stop whining and waiting. She would believe that good things will happen to her. She would not tolerate Kurt's hurting her anymore. She would demand to be loved. She would believe she is worthy. She would make works of art. She would stay focused on that daily. She would not give up. She would enjoy each moment, find herself laughing and smiling easily. She would trust. She would stop punishing herself for not being young. She would be beautiful. She would be herself. She would exude sexuality. She would be loving. She would be a catch because of it. She would be the woman she wants to be. Warm. Smart and lovely to be with. She would know that difficulties, such as money and lack of love, never last forever. That creative blocks break. That friendships and beauty abound if you show up for them. That she would let herself be loved.

That, she decided as the sun beat onto her balcony and the blue of the sea dazzled its light, was what was next.

CHAPTER 33

Before she left for Uruguay, her young student and she had been crossing the street in New York. "Why do I have to go to university? You've taught me everything."

She laughed, while also thinking that this boy was a born ladies man. "Well, maybe you've got a point. Oscar Wilde said, Education is an admirable thing, but it is well to remember from time to time that nothing that is worth knowing can be taught. But it's a joke," she answered. "You'll learn how to think. You'll meet interesting people. New Books. New ways. New ideas of whom you can be."

But inside she was proud because she had taught him that

knowledge does reside in our own eyes, our own mistakes, our own images and the exploration of them. We will come to the center from where we begin, in other words, we will only get to know the truths by digging within, while looking and listening without. What's important are the questions, not always the answers, but let him find out for himself so she said nothing.

But then she thought otherwise. "Whitehead said the danger of science," she continued, "is that you can stare at the stars so long, you stop seeing them. In other words, limited viewing can be stultifying. The breakthroughs come when you're not looking or catch the light from the side of your eye or, in other words, when you shake things up. You hear a sentence. You see something you had not seen before. You make an intuitive leap. You know that anyway," she said smiling at his tall beautiful intelligence, "from having written so long."

"Explain it," he said, "another way."

"David Whyte, and he is not a poet I particularly like, but I like this, wrote, Give up all the other worlds/except the one to which you belong."

Her student looked over at her but she was busy, thinking. She was thinking that she herself belonged to the world of the mind. She gave that to her students, the ones who wanted that connection. She also belonged to the world of sexual exuding, which was only a willingness to love. Man. Woman. Dog. Seal. Clients. Her own work. Sun.

They had gone, the three women in Uruguay, she, Sara and Darlene, who was Sara's friend, to the Spanish Shabbat where the Uruguayans who were regulars told the women visitors that their synagogue refused to hire a rabbi. The attendants of the Shabbat wanted to be Jews, but not lectured as Jews. They sang songs in Hebrew and Mira did not understand the words, but they were songs of praise and something alchemical was happening within her as she participated. She was being cleansed and renewed. Small children ran around looking for snacks, mothers looked madly in love with these little beings, children looked as in love with their mothers. The men practiced their English with Mira and her friends and the sound of their lilting words, Spanish into English, was music and spiritual in itself.

After the Shabbat, the three women walked in and by the warm night's seacoast and Sara took them to her house and they met her 84 year old husband with his lit up dark eyes and enormous stomach and Mira noticed the love between them. There was a reverence to it, as if they knew it was to be gently honored, even when they could not stand each other. Mira felt compassion and admiration for women like Sara who were able to love and were able to give up something of their fascistic independence to do so. There was humility in not expecting the man to be perfect and Mira decided to remember this. Kurt was not perfect and why should he be? Neither was Mira.

There was a reverence in how Mira had loved Kurt, admiring how elegantly he dressed in cravats and expensive shirts and jackets for their dates, for how they planned their evenings with films, plays and music to give them both happiness. There was mirth in their joy together and there was mirth in the shoreline here in Punta del Este in Uruguay. There was reverence in Sara's attention to the writing Sara wanted Mira to do, in the way she flew Mira down to help her tell her story. They were both engaged in reverence for her story.

Of course Kurt feared Mira. He knew only too well that, for him, women are explosive, energetic, emotional, and imperfect. They frighten order and the rational.

When she thought about it, she was the one people listened to when they were meeting people, she was the woman whose gravitas got the attention, except for his little games which confused people. She was the one who rubbed her hands on his chest, and touched him, and smiled in delight at him. She was the one who gave him pleasure in bed. She was the one who got upset when there were other women around because she wanted him for herself. She was the one who made a fool of herself in this way. She was the one who burst out in her needs and insecurities. She was the one who had countless friends and interests and ran around helping people as much as she could. She was the one who sometimes couldn't speak when they first saw each other because she was overcome with emotion. She was the one whose body had flaws, and whose face had flaws and who often was not dressed as he would like. She was the one who got very strident about whatever she believed. She was the one who kept prodding him, Come out from your lockdown and let us love, live.

Probably he hated it, he who had barricaded himself into his jewel box with his chefs. Why didn't Mira just enjoy her visits to his jewel box? Why did she want them to make mistakes together?

Don't ask what the world needs, Howard Thurston wrote. What the world needs are people who have come alive.

CHAPTER 34

At night in her hotel room, she could not sleep. She thought about Lucia. As Mira tossed and turned, she imagined she was talking about her at the eulogy. She could not fathom that Lucia was no longer here. No more deconstructing on those impromptu visits upstairs. And, even to make impromptu visits in New York was an unusual intimacy. Everyone in New York is too busy for each other.

Mira tried to watch TV in her hotel room, on the crisp white bed, but every show was violence. She had to turn it off.

She focused, instead, on the violence of how Kurt did not contact her. It was unforgivable to her. She always had time to contact him. She thought of other men she knew who were not in constant contact with their significant others. She tried not to vilify Kurt but she was hurt. Maybe she should end these repetitions of rejection, their lack of evolution, as Whitehead would say.

She had a physical pain in her heart. She did not know where it was coming from. She had to grab the rail carefully as she walked down the hotel steps to breakfast the next morning. She felt like she could faint. Perhaps the coldness she felt in her body was what he had been feeling toward her. Perhaps she knew there was no home with him. Perhaps the pain in her heart was she knew she must begin her life again, as she had as a young girl.

Perhaps she needed someone to care for her. She had never thought like that and yet everywhere there were people caring, people seemed to know that caring was a necessary part of life. Perhaps the pain in her heart was the striving, the constant striving toward what she wanted but feeling that, if she continued in this way, she would never achieve it.

Sara obliquely tried to encourage her to look away from Kurt. "Don't you realize that young man sat beside you at lunch? Carlos, my husband, thinks you are pretty. The men at the synagogue came over to talk to you."

Mira had not noticed, busy in her repetition.

CHAPTER 35

She did not want to write the eulogy while away or do anything that required focus. Here in Punta by the sea, she just wanted, she realized, to be receptive. Here she was taking in beauty and air and love and being rejiggered. The sun on the water, the birds, the open vistas, the beaches. Her cells were reshifting toward something else. Here she was away from unhappiness and over-exertion. Here she was just in the moment. And even if it hurt a bit, to slow down enough, for her body to assert itself, then it was still right.

She was being, not doing.

Sara's husband spent most of his time sitting on the balcony. "I love it here in the winter," he said, sitting in his chair, looking out over the sea. Apparently it got cooler and more intimate in winter, he explained, more open. His wife and dog sat with him. He drank his strong coffee.

Duras ended up somewhere like this. Mira thought Deauville by the sea was where she wrote The Lover.

To write what is deepest. A love. A forbidden love.

"I will never marry or live with you," Kurt said.

"I love you but I am not in love with you," he said.

How she so quickly agreed in her soul to be deprived. She must have inherently felt there was something wrong with her and Kurt had seen it at once.

She dreamed she died with Lucia. She didn't believe the dream portended that she was dying. Nothing would be that neat and, if it was, it would prove nothing. Everything was random in life and that was why Kurt tried to control it.

But she did believe one had to end something to begin something new.

Something must die.

Sara talked of unspeakable loneliness as a child, without her parents, living in a children's house as a baby and child, with only one caretaker for 24 children. She hated the nights. She had no one to console her or comfort her. There was no protection. Her husband had been the one to protect her with his constancy, his body, his body of love, and she could travel from there.

Mira wondered what it was that protected her. She told herself it was not expecting too much and going to what uplifted her. She must have wanted, as Whitehead said, to upwardly trend. In the areas of the soul.

But the soul operates differently than the mind. The mind rationalizes, wants material proof of matters that may not even be germane. The soul will inexorably stop for love, if we let the soul run the show.

CHAPTER 36

Kurt sent her an email that ended, Sleep tight and don't let the bedbugs bite. He wrote her of dinners he was going to, tennis games and of a weekend in Miami at a spa with his son. He did not tell her he missed her.

Sara remarked on how Kurt did not help her with money, how he was not there. Sara remarked he must have more compatibility with a woman his own age, like her. More compatibility than with all the younger women he had been with. Or lives with.

"You are perfect for me," he had announced the first time they met, surprising her. She had also been struck that he had not wondered out loud if he was perfect for her.

"You are much more than a girlfriend," he said another time. He knew when to give some lead and when to rein it in.

She wrestled with her decision about what she wanted for the future. She was with Sara sitting outside in the café Sara wrote in. Mira was purring just to be outside, just to be with this kind woman by the sea, searching for that abandoned child in herself who had been crying to be held and heard.

Sara said, "I feel it is not finished. You will be with him."

Mira looked into the sunlight for an answer.

Sara said, "I feel he does not like your being away."

"Perhaps," Mira answered. "I am happy here."

"It frightens him," she said.

Let him do something about it, Mira thought. If he cannot, I cannot. I have to be in the sun of someone's life.

"I just don't want to be hurt by his insensitivities anymore," she said to Sara.

"What do you mean?" she asked.

"If he refuses to communicate with me, what is the point?"

Sara did not respond and simply said, "You will figure it out."

"Yes, you're right. I will. Anyway, life always plays a hand," and she could not take her eyes off the sea in the horizon.

CHAPTER 37

Her young student now had his own fulsome life. He devoured poetry and kisses from his girlfriend. He waited to hear if Harvard had accepted him.

Meanwhile she continued to meet him every Saturday at noon in a coffee shop near his bus from the Bronx.

"Do you need to have a difficult life to be a writer?" she remembered him asking her when he was 12 years old. They were just getting to know each other.

"Why? Have you had a difficult life?" she replied.

"My parents married each other twice."

"A lot of writers have had difficult lives, it's true. You feel more. But it's not a necessity."

But mostly he asked about books. Sometimes they talked about romance. Once when he was only thirteen, she had been angry at Kurt.

"Why?" the boy asked. "What did he do?"

She showed him one of many insensitive emails Kurt had sent. Mira could hardly teach that day she was so distraught with Kurt's flippancy.

Her student read the email.

"He's just kidding you," Senegal said.

And at that moment she knew he was right.

"Maybe you should be coaching me," she said.

If she fell in love with a book, it was her student whom she told about it. Got him a copy. She forgot so often he was a child because his intellect was creative, alive. He is one of us, she thought. I am working with one of us. He will go out into the world and know what is meaningful. It is in his blood.

When he was very young, they shared salads.

When older, coffees and macaroons.

His mother liked the attention she gave him, the constant books, the discussion. The mother must have known he had a curious mind and needed constant feeding.

When he was still a small boy, Mira once took him out for

a steak dinner for his birthday. "The mafia owns this place," he explained to her, waving his fork around. It was not the steak; it was the stories in his mind and around him that he ingested.

He never called her about writing advice. He called her only once to ask how to make a lychee martini, a drink she said she loved. He was thirteen.

"That may not be my role in your life, to tell you how to mix drinks," she said.

He laughed.

Another time she was again lamenting how Kurt was difficult. "Why is that?" she asked.

He was now sixteen. "You chose to date an alien," he said. "You just want someone you can't understand."

Even this young boy knew she could not be tamed by natural causes.

CHAPTER 38

She was once again sitting over the sea, but in New York. They had driven to a place in Coney Island, of all venues. A restaurant over the boardwalk.

"I wanted to see it," said Bill, Lucia's quasi-relative. "One reads about it. Even in poetry."

They were in Brighton Beach, specifically, which is Russian. If it were Kurt, his eyes would be traveling sideways all the time to look at the Russian women in their off the shoulder tops and powerful eyes.

Bill was looking at Mira.

"Do you want a special vodka?" he asked.

"Sure."

He laughed. "God knows what you'll get. I'm not letting you drive, though."

She smiled.

Kurt hadn't answered her when she said she wanted communication when she was lonely in Uruguay. Hadn't even bothered to write an email. He wouldn't even give her that little bone. So she had stopped writing him. She had stopped begging. And when he asked why her silence, she said, she was tired of silence, even when communicating. She told him to find another date. The way he fitted her into his life was eminently replaceable. New York was full of women, like her, she didn't say, who would accept anything. It made her sad, she did write, and she loved him, but he didn't need her. He told her he respected her, he told her he loved her, he told her a lot of things. But what he didn't realize was he was telling her by email and that was precisely why she could not rescind.

Somehow she now had a chance at being touched.

She cursorily looked over at Bill, and his beautiful face, sitting with his back to the sea. Here she was. It wasn't warm, not Uruguay, but they were by the sea. He had driven them.

"Have you been to Cornwall?" she asked.

"Of course."

She didn't say she hadn't been and wanted to.

"So is everything done with Lucia's apartment?" she asked.

"Yes, I dropped off most of her belongings at my mother's." He reached into his pocket. "I saved this for you. I actually thought it was the prettiest and would look far better on you than my mother or any of her friends."

He handed her a small ring that had rather large and stunning amber and amethyst stones. She had never seen that combination of stones before.

"It's lovely. It's unusual."

"That's why I thought it would suit you."

Look, Mira, he's not giving you a ring he bought.

"Funny, not sure it looks like her," she said.

"Well probably one of her suitors bought it for her," he said. "She always attracted men."

"Yes she used to like to talk about relationships. Did you like her husband?" she asked.

"Herman? He was very energetic in that he worked so hard. But he was a hypochondriac and needed a lot of attention in that way. A bit tedious in a way and apparently hot tempered. A handful. Another survivor. But he left her fairly well off and I think he loved her. Not sure how good he was at loving." He looked out at the water. "Not sure how good any of us are at loving."

She sipped her vodka.

"Why? Have you had a checkered love life?" she asked.

"Hasn't everyone?"

She had that feeling with him, that feeling that she did not want to leave him. Her body, without asking her, had said yes to him. She could touch him, if she knew him better. It was his face. It was handsome but knowing. Had humor in it and a focus.

"Your business card said you are in the British government," she said. "MI6?"

He laughed. "If you want."

"Are you an MP whose recent sex scandal landed you here?"

"I don't think so."

If only, she at this age, could be the woman in the recent sex scandal.

She went to the ladies room and it was one of those mirrors that make one look thinner and thus taller, more glamorous. Maybe it's not the mirror. What difference does it make?

She came back and sat down and put the ring on.

"I didn't realize Lucia had such small hands," she said. "It fits."

He looked down at her hand. "Yes."

She stared out at the sea. He looked at his phone not in a

panicky way or in a way of avoidance but in a way where they were comfortable together. There is lunch and there is the consistency of work. Eventually they would find out all the literal matters of each other's lives.

The boats in the water sat tranquilly and spoke of sun-filled lives.

Lucia. She would be glad she was here with Bill.

"Did you find anything that surprised you when you cleaned out her apartment?" she asked.

"That ring. I don't think Herman gave that to her. It doesn't look like him. Too subtle."

"Where do you think she got it?"

"Someone in her life must have been subtle," he said. "Sophisticated in his taste." He laughed. "Maybe my father."

"That's a thought."

"Well someone. Someone she loved enough to keep it. I don't think my father would do that to my mother anyway, thank God."

"What else did you find of interest?"

"She didn't have much, really. Books, as you know. Old piano music. Photos of the past. Not the long past but her marriage. Nothing really, oh, except your books. She had all your books."

Oh God, Mira thought.

"Which I read."

"Oh."

"They are brave," he said. "You say a lot of truths."

"Well I don't know if I believe half of what I write myself. It comes and it goes. One writes in a persona," she said. "And maybe the persona changes. Did you read her book?" she said quickly. She did not want to talk about her books. And she liked that he did not ask that god-awful question, "Is the story true?" Is it possible he is smart enough to know that all stories are true and not true?

"No," he said. "I did not read her book. I heard it all growing up. Oh," he added, "she had a wonderful poem that summed up her life I thought." He pulled a piece of paper out of his pocket. His pockets seemed to be filled with things. What would Freud say?

"It's by Wallace Stevens," he said. He unfolded the paper.

"He and I have the same birthday," she volunteered.

"That's interesting," he said and put on his glasses. "Listen,
'I do not know which to prefer,
The beauty of inflections
Or the beauty of innuendos,
The blackbird whistling
Or just after.'"

"Someone," he said, "you, should read that at her memorial."

CHAPTER 39

In Uruguay, she had been sitting with Darlene and Sara at a restaurant looking out over the bay. They were drinking caporescas and the sun had gone down, it was dark, and they were eating hors d'oeuvres and they were discussing life. An Italian waiter flitted about. How had he ended up in Uruguay, she wondered. It seemed a long way from Italy. What was he leaving or going to?

The women wanted to know about Kurt.

She explained he lived with young chefs.

"Is he sleeping with them?" they asked.

"He probably wants to but he is a lot older than they are. Who wants to sleep with someone that old when you are young?"

"It's not the point," Sara said. "He is living with another woman. That is why he doesn't want you. He knows how to take care of himself."

"Sounds like it," Darlene laughed.

Sara looked sorrowfully over at Mira, as if to say, you are a fool. The way Mira's students whom she had fixed up with his son had looked at her after they met Kurt.

Whitehead said our goal is to live better, which to him meant bringing about an increase in satisfaction. That same satisfaction came from instability, which leads to growth.

Change. The new.

An increase in satisfaction would be being involved with kind and loving people, only spending time with them, she realized.

She had had no stability and it was true she had never been attracted to it. When Mark and other men had tried to seduce her with the promise of it, she was like a horse who reared away. Perhaps she took instability too seriously.

From her hotel, she had written Kurt that they should go to Uruguay together. "Wonderful idea," he responded. "Perhaps I can rent a villa."

Always the big man. But she did not believe him. He liked to posture.

"I always wondered what Uruguay is like," he said.

That was before she sent the email asking for contact to which she got no response. He could rent a villa, but not answer her back. How much she wanted to be answered back.

She had longed for the sea. And found it. An Israeli woman in the seminar class she took who wanted to write about her inner child led her out of one life into the instability of the next.

Magnetism.

When Mira left them for the airport, Sara's husband, sitting in the driver's seat of their car, said to her, "It is like we are old friends."

Sara's dog kissing Mira as she left.

The sea gold and blue in the sun. Magnetism. Music.

Sara said, "Carlos has to have sex twice a week. He Is 84."

"But that is good, Sara."

Magnetism. Carlos teased Sara. Sat with his cane and dark burning eyes of joy. The dog whimpered when Carlos was not in the room.

Sara needed to write the story that Lucia wrote about surviving suffering. Different story, but the truth.

Mira gave the eulogy at the synagogue. Because of Lucia's book, two hundred people were there, to Mira's shock.

Mira spoke of Lucia's love of life, survival, and her creativity to keep going.

After she stepped down off the podium, Mira felt relieved. It had taken much energy to write about her, much energy to put herself on show like that with her feelings for Lucia.

At the reception, she shook hands with many people.

She learned how much Lucia had done and how many people loved her. Obviously her aloneness was her own doing.

Bill too was talking with many people. He looked confident in a dark suit and white shirt.

Finally, he came over to her. "Well, quite a success," he said, "if one can call a memorial a success."

She said nothing. She was so tired.

"Yes. Well, what are you doing now?" he asked.

"I don't know."

"Well come out with me and have a drink. I have to stop by an agency and pick up something on the way. Do you mind?"

"The CIA Agency?"

"God, writers and their imaginations. No, a travel agency."

"Oh. Going somewhere?"

"Yes. I want to buy a house in South America."

She stood looking at him stunned.

"You know it?" he asked.

"I just came back from there. Remember? From Uruguay. It is beautiful." Was this a joke? Of Lucia's?

"Lucia loved Peru," he said.

"I know. She went to Machu Picchu," Mira said.

"Where were you?" he asked.

"Montevideo and around Punte del Este."

"How funny," he said.

She thought she couldn't breathe.

"I must say at times you say the oddest things," he said, smiling, "but so what? Come on let's get out of here. We sent her off well. It's our job to finish our own lives out well, I suppose."

"That's something she would say."

She really wanted to say; You say some odd things yourself. But she was too joyful inside.

Everything seemed at that moment, magnetized. She might as well go for it, go for broke.

"Let me think up somewhere beautiful," she said, "to go have a drink."

She remembered the Chinese poet, Lu-An, Ask until there

is nothing left to ask.

Bill looked at her. She looked at her new ring. And then he nodded, silently. A sea of feeling rushed forward inside her. And then she knew, that sea, that eros, that music, always would be rushing. She just had to stay still for it.

ABOUT THE AUTHOR

British born, Montreal raised, New York City honed, JACQUELINE GAY WALLEY, under the pen name Gay Walley, has been publishing short stories since 1988 and published her first novel, *Strings Attached*, with University Press of Mississippi (1999), which was a Finalist for the Pirates Alley/Faulkner Award and earned a Writer's Voice Capricorn Award and the Paris Book Festival Award. *The Erotic Fire of the Unattainable: Aphorisms on Love, Art and the Vicissitudes of Life* was published by IML Publications in 2007 and was reissued by Skyhorse Publishing 2015. This book, *The Erotic Fire of the Unattainable* was a finalist for the Paris Book Festival Award and from this, she wrote a screenplay for the film, *The Unattainable Story* (2016) with actor, Harry Hamlin, which premiered at the Mostra Film Festival in Sao Paolo, Brazil. Walley also wrote a screenplay for director Frank Vitale's docufiction feature film, *Erotic Fire of the Unattainable: Longing to be Found* (2020), which was featured in Brooklyn Film Festival, Sarasota Film Festival, Cinequest Film & Creativity Festival in San Jose, ReadingFilmFest, and American Fringe in Paris (2020). Her novel, *Lost in Montreal* (2013) was published by Incanto Press, along with the novel, *Duet*, which was written with Kurt Haber. Walley's e-books, *How to Write Your First Novel*, *Save Your One Person Business from Extinction*, and *The Smart Guide to Business Writing* are featured on Bookboon, as well as *How to Keep Calm and Carry on Without Money* and

How to be Beautiful available on Amazon. In 2013, her play *Love, Genius and a Walk* opened in the Midtown Festival, New York, and was nominated for 6 awards including best playwright, in 2018, it also played in London at The Etcetera Theatre above The Oxford Arms pub as well as at three other pub theatres. It is scheduled to open in 2021 in Theatro Techni in London. In October 2021, Jacqueline Gay Walley's 6 novel *Venus as She Ages* Collection – *Strings Attached* (second edition, under her pen name, Gay Walley), *To Any Lengths, Prison Sex, The Bed You Lie In, Write She Said*, and *Magnetism* – is being launched worldwide through IML Publications and distributed by Ingram.

Since IML's humble erratic beginnings, the mascot, which has reverently danced across our newsletter, the watermarks of the website, the original interiors, and now these front and back pages, is a graphic symbol of the Kalahari San Bushmen's Trickster God, the praying mantis, who has forever—or for as long as they can remember—been inspiring the mythological stories of these First People who nomadically walk the earth whenever they can, as our nomad authors write their way through life.

CPSIA information can be obtained
at www.ICGtesting.com
Printed in the USA
BVHW081242290921
617680BV00008B/354